Jack Russelled to Death

Cavaliered to Death

Bichoned to Death

Shepherded to Death

Doodled to Death

Corgied to Death

Aussied to Death

Dachshund to Death (coming Nov. 2023)

Labradored to Death (coming Spring 2024)

AUSSIED TO DEATH

A BARKVIEW MYSTERY

C.B. WILSON

For Debbie (Dee) Kaler
the sister I prayed for

CONTENTS

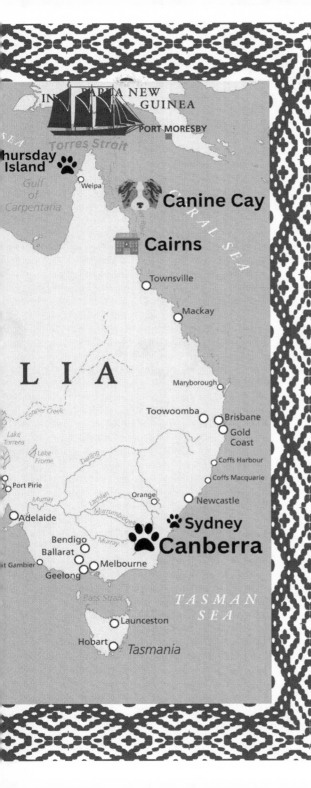

CHARACTERS, HUMAN

Andrew-Downs, Theodore (TAD): Bartender at Canine Cay resort.

Ashley: Canine Cay guest. Bridget, a Yorkie, is her dog.

Banning-Smith, Rog: Canine Cay Park Ranger. Torres Strait Islander. Bull, a Bull Dog, is his dog.

Barklay, Charlotte (Aunt Char): Mayor of Barkview, dog psychiatrist on *Throw Him a Bone*. Renny, a champion Cavalier King Charles Spaniel, is her dog.

Cathaway, Bart: British Solicitor. Duke, a Cavalier King Charles, is his dog.

Cooper-Davis, Emma: Manager, Canine Cay Resort.

Cooper, Dylan (Coop): Emma's brother. Runs Canine Cay Winery.

Cooper, Meryl: Emma's sister. Runs Canine Cay Pearl Farm. Pearl, a Cobberdoodle, is her dog.

Hawl, Russ: Cat's husband. FBI consultant. Owns Blue Diamond Security.

Hawl-Wright, Catalina "Cat": General Manager at KDOG. A cat person living in Barkview.

Holmes, Alice & Virgil: Canine Cay guests from Sydney.

Lily: Meryl's assistant.

Lugger T: A Torres Strait Islander. Bush Pilot. Lizzie, an Australian Shepherd, is his dog.

Moore, Jennifer: Barkview Librarian.

Morgan-Blackman, Holland (Holly): Canine Cay Guest.

Morgan, Colonel Mathew: Court-martialed Colonel.

Schmidt, Gregory (Uncle G): Barkview's police chief. Max and Maxine, silver-point German Shepherds, are his dogs.

White, Lena & Harris: Canine Cay guests from Sydney.

Wynne, Sandy: Cat's assistant and computer whiz. Jack, a Jack Russell Terrier, is her dog.

Zachary, (Z): Coop's assistant at the vineyard.

CHARACTERS, CANINE

🐾 Bull: Rog's Bull Dog.

🐾 Bridget: Ashley's Yorkie.

🐾 Duke: Bart Cathaway's champion Cavalier King Charles Spaniel.

🐾 Jack: Sandy's Jack Russell Terrier.

🐾 Lizzie: Lugger T's Australian Shepherd.

🐾 Pearl: Meryl's Cobberdoodle.

🐾 Renny: Aunt Char's champion Cavalier King Charles Spaniel.

CHAPTER 1

What's not to love about an exotic honeymoon getaway on a remote island on the Great Barrier Reef? Did I mention that the island is Canine Cay? You guessed it—only I can travel seven thousand, two hundred and twenty-seven miles from Barkview (not that I'm counting) and end up on the dog-friendliest island in Australia. I don't hate dogs. In fact, after my last canine near-calamity, I have developed a true appreciation for a pooch's protective predispositions. I'd just hoped not to hear a single headache-inducing bark for two short weeks.

This *woof* struck like a sledgehammer on my what-the-heck-time-is-it fogged brain. I peered toward the sliding-glass door, blinded by a single strip of sunlight peeking between the blackout blinds.

I tried to nudge my new husband, Russ, but crazy morning person that he was, he'd already vacated, time zone impervious. The bedside clock glowed 7 a.m. Australian Eastern time, which translated into 2 p.m. yesterday in Barkview. Never good with less than seven hours of shut eye a night, I hadn't slept in two days. Talk about jet lag. Every blink felt like sandpaper scraping my eyelids. The twenty-two hours flying and three plane changes remained a blur. Since finding Paula's killer had been stressful and our impromptu wedding a whirlwind, you'd think I would've just crashed on the luxurious 787. Not! I watched every peaceful rise and fall of Russ's well-defined linebacker shoulders and that stray dark hair on his forehead until the plane landed in Sydney. My husband practically carried me, bleary-eyed and dog-tired, to the connecting flight to Cairns. Three hours later, we climbed aboard a beat-up, single-engine bush plane for a race-against-the-sunset flight to Canine Cay. Not that the duct tape holding the propeller to the plane bothered me or anything. After our customs fiasco in Sydney, I didn't want to know how Russ had conjured up our colorful Melanesian pilot, dressed in a bright Hawaiian shirt, who'd introduced himself as Lugger T, a proud Torres Strait Islander. I was even too wiped out to care when Lugger asked me my weight, gave me a you-can't-be-for-real look when I answered, and weighed me on the airport freight scale to prove his point. Was he testing me, or was the man just ornery? Seriously, what intelligent man asks a woman her weight after a celebration where champagne flowed followed by a long overseas flight? Water weight is a killer. That's my story, and I'm sticking to it.

That embarrassment dealt with, we finally approached the small plane. Except a merle-spotted, stub-tailed Australian Shepherd with patchwork-stocking legs and a snow-white ascot blocked my entry.

"Lizzie, step aside an' bid g'day to me mates." Lugger's heavily accented words couldn't possibly be English.

Russ seemed to get it. After a runway-clearing sneeze, he said, "G'day to you too." He motioned for me to pet the dog.

I did. Better me than him. Seriously, only I could marry a

man allergic to dogs. Long, multicolored fur strands wrapped around my hand like a glove. Ugh! I tried a get-the-goo-off handshake, which sort of worked until the dog brushed against my black stretch pants. Globs of fur stuck right to me as if I were Velcro. I didn't panic. I calmly picked off the most prominent offenders. My last Corgi adventure must've desensitized me—not that I'd admit it.

I frowned at the Aussie, who I would have sworn saw everything in a single, perceptive blue-eyed glance, frighteningly similar to her owner, who observed my every move with a calculated intelligence I found unnerving.

I ran my fingers through my rumpled shoulder-length hair. "Your, uh, Aussie is beautiful. I bet there are a lot of them in Australia."

"Naw. Aussies be Yanks. She be a *suh-pryz* from a mate. Bes' watcher in 'Stralya," Lugger insisted.

Huh? Was that a question or a statement? The Aussie accent really made my head spin. Russ didn't miss a beat. "A guard dog? How's that working for you?" My husband had to be as tired as I was. Why else would he ask such a strange question?

Lugger's dark eyes glittered with mischief as he patted a familiar bump on his hip. "Useful."

I shivered. I couldn't help myself. The man carried a concealed weapon. I recognized the bump only because Russ carried at home too. Was Lugger in law enforcement or a criminal? Even I knew the gun laws in Australia were strict.

"I didn't know Aussies were good guard dogs." Was a dog my answer to protection?

"Aussies be smart herdin' dogs. Mi Lizzie be disc masta."

I frowned. "A what?"

"A Frisbee champion," Russ replied. Sweat dampened the

rim of his Barkview Pickleball baseball cap. Good to know he felt the humidity too.

The dog's pacing did indicate she possessed a lot of energy.

"She be a fierce protecta too." Lugger scratched the dog's head. Lizzie leaned into him, just about purring.

If I listened hard enough, I could piece together a general meaning to his words.

Russ squeezed my hand. "Lugger, quit telling my wife your stories."

Wife! Okay, the man really did know how to divert my attention. Add a suggestive baby-blue glance, and I was lost. Married life really was perfect.

I breathed easier. Kind of. There was more to this. The look Russ and Lugger exchanged could only be called familiar. No. It had to be my only-half-coherent brain. How could they possibly know each other?

I wiped the perspiration off my face with my signature leopard-print scarf. Right this minute I couldn't care less if anyone saw my scar. Summertime in Barkview didn't have humidity this oppressive. I could hardly breathe. I climbed into the back seat while Russ and Lugger loaded our luggage and a cardboard box of something unrecognizable.

In a cloud of fur, the dog jumped inside the plane and sat sphinx-style on the seat beside me. Her paws crossed, she sniffed in my direction and buried her nose.

Was I that offensive? Sure, I'd been wearing the same yoga pants and comfy, long-sleeved blue shirt that Russ said matched my eyes since yesterday, or was that the day before yesterday? I clenched my arms at my sides anyway.

I glanced at Russ, sneezing in the doorway. So much for the series of allergy shots diminishing his dog sensitivity. Note to self: carry allergy pills with me everywhere. Who knew we'd need them on vacation? Apparently, Lugger did. He handed

Russ a packet of something and a bottle of water. No doubt he'd had other passengers with the same issue.

Russ downed the contents and settled into the copilot's seat as if it were his living room recliner. Russ, a pilot? He'd never said a word about it to me. Not that I expected him to tell me every little thing about himself. I hadn't shared my many embarrassing moments with him either. Much as I craved answers, even I admitted that some things are better left unsaid. Being a pilot, though? That seemed significant.

My intuition tingled as the small plane lifted off on the last leg of our journey. The steady propeller hum lulled me into oblivion until Lugger said, "Reckon we'll make the Cay late arvo. That be afternoon to you Yanks."

"Why does that matter?" The fireball sun poised just above the hills framing Cairns caught my eye out the window.

"There be no landin' lights." Not that it seemed to matter to Lugger. The man's expertise showed in his ease at the controls. Besides, there was no way Russ would endanger me.

"Tell me about the island." Other than the surrounding reef being one of the seven wonders of the natural world, I knew nothing about this northern island located in the Coral Sea. Russ had surprised me with the trip before my first cup of coffee the morning after our wedding.

"You'll need a passport and your PADI dive card. Sandy packed everything else you'll need." Of course, he'd drawn Sandy Wynne, my ever-perky blonde production assistant at KDOG, into the conspiracy. She loved a good adventure as much as I did and knew me better than myself at times.

"I can't leave the station." As the general manager of KDOG, Barkview's premier TV station, every day I faced an inbox teetering like the Leaning Tower of Pisa. I cringed just thinking about that mess.

"Your aunt has it covered," Russ replied.

"Aunt Char is the mayor. She can't possibly run Barkview and the TV station."

Russ just smiled. Who was I kidding? Although she was pushing sixty, Aunt Char possessed an energy and cool competence that made my concerns sound ridiculous. Further objections faded as an airport limo picked us up thirty minutes later. I don't know how he'd arranged everything, but we were off for two weeks to a scuba diver's paradise.

"The legend o' the Cay tells the tale of the great dingo spirit," Lugger explained.

"A dog spirit?" Talk about a nightmare.

"Yeah. And a powerful one at that."

"What exactly does this so-called spirit do?" Curiosity stirred, penetrating the cobwebs in my head. Legends intrigued me.

Lugger's silver-toothed smile reflected in the glass. "The Aboriginals say the great spirit be a shift changer, both dingo and human."

A dogman? Russ didn't completely hide his amusement. Blame it on fatigue. I'd walked right into that one. "Come on."

"Fair dinkum," Lugger insisted. "The spirit be the protecta of the Cay treasure."

I crossed my arms. Even I saw the mischief in Lugger's dark eyes.

"The map." He patted a colorful piece of paper sticking out of his breast pocket. "It be 'bout believin'."

Believing in fantasy? Maybe there was more to this story, but I was here on my honeymoon. Did I really want to know? Of course I did. Treasure hunting drove me, the crazier the quest the better. All-too-familiar anticipation stirred. "What exactly is this so-called treasure?"

"A lost packet o' diamonds."

Not another diamond hunt! I ignored Russ's you-had-to-ask head shake. "The Cay is internationally known for pearls."

"That it is. An' some beauts too."

Before I could ask for clarification, the plane dipped below the puffy clouds, revealing a picture-perfect purple-pink canvas painted across the sky. I stared in awe at the azure water broken only by the reef's darker outline. OMG! Photos didn't even come close to showing the raw beauty of the underwater coral formations lining the shore. They called for exploration.

"Looky there." The plane dove.

I saw it then, some distance away: the silhouette of a proud, long-tailed dog outlined in rock. The collar area and underbelly twinkled like pavé diamonds in the fading light. I fumbled with my phone and took a picture. The folks in Barkview would love this.

"The Cay be known for Cay Pearls," Lugger explained. "The farm be inside the tail. Them golden jewels sparkle like diamonds."

Not exactly. I'd examined both the Smithsonian's magnificent Shepard Diamond and its match, the recently-recovered Douglas Diamond. Although rumored to be bewitchingly luminescent with an inner fire, no pearl could compete with that golden legend. Naturally, a blingaholic like me was willing to test it. "I'll need to see that to believe it."

Lugger's knowing nod accepted the challenge. "The giant clam pearls are the size of a man's fist." The little plane swooped to the right as the man illustrated the size with his dominant fist.

He righted the plane before I could brace myself, my eyes no doubt the size of saucers. A pearl the size of a man's fist would be a sight to see. "What is the story about the diamonds?"

"No story. Fact is, a plane carryin' a parcel o' diamonds from the Bank of Java bound for the Sultan of Delhi was shot down in Broome in June 1942. The stones were called the Dakota Diamonds."

"Dakota?" We were a long way from North or South Dakota.

"Yeah. The plane was a Douglas C-47 known as a Dakota. The diamonds were never recovered."

"Broome is twenty-five hundred kilometers from Canine Cay." I heard Russ's dry comment loud and clear.

"Yeah-nah." Lugger patted the map. "The great dingo spirit protects the treasure waiting for the true believer."

So much for a real treasure hunt. That Lugger believed it I did not doubt. Me? I ignored Russ's I-told-you-so look, instead focusing on the encroaching darkness and a new fear. Would we be able to land?

We arrived just as the last rays illuminated what could only be described as a swath of concrete dissecting a dry pasture. Cows even grazed on the periphery to prove it. The only light glowed like a beacon from a weathered, two-story, A-frame barn at the end of the runway. Lugger didn't seem to mind. He banked, then dropped the nose, and landed with a precision indicating years of practice. He popped the bottle top off a XXXX Lager and offered another to Russ as the plane stopped. "Stubby, mate?"

Russ declined. Not a beer fan, I did as well.

"Suit yourselves." Lugger took a long swallow. Lizzie slipped her head beneath my arms and licked Lugger's bottle. Really, a beer dog?

Twin lights like beady eyes floated just above ground level in the fading light until a turquoise-and-white, open-air vehicle appeared beside the barn. Rounded like the roof of a

8

classic 1970s Volkswagen Bug with four wide tires, it looked ideally suited to an off-road adventure.

Lizzie bolted from the plane with an exuberant bark to meet an athletic blonde dressed in a black pencil skirt and a rolled-sleeved khaki blouse. The woman embraced the dog, who licked her face. Double ick! Why did dogs face-lick anyway?

Eventually, the woman straightened her skirt, pulled off a stray Aussie hair or two, and strode to our aircraft. "G'day, Mr. and Mrs. Hawl. Welcome to Canine Cay." I noticed her hiking boots as she handed Russ and me aluminum water bottles. "I'm Emma, the resort manager."

Her charming accent was definitely foreign, but entirely understandable. I glanced at Lugger, who just inclined his head, chewing on something—I didn't want to know what. I breathed easier.

"Let's get to it," Emma urged us. "Chef has *lobbies* on the barbie prepared for you at the Look Out. Best to try to stay the course tonight to fast-track the jet lag."

I frowned at Russ. "Stay awake as late as you can," he explained. "It's the best way to adjust to the local time."

As if he were an international travel expert. Or was he? Wasn't the FBI restricted to working in the US? "What are '*lobbies*?'" I asked.

Emma smiled. "Locally sourced freshwater crayfish. Contrary to your yank version, ours boast a delicate, earthy flavor. Tonight, they are served as a starter with crusty bread and a lemon twist."

Spoken like a true foodie. Yum. My mouth watered at the thought. What wasn't to love about local delicacies? "Are you a chef?"

"Nah. Just a local gal with an appetite."

To nibble. How else could she maintain that slim, petite figure?

"You will appreciate Chef's local farm-to-table cuisine." Emma gestured for us to follow her to the vehicle. "Your luggage will join you at your lodge." She waited for Russ and me to climb into the back seat before adding, "Now, don't you be takin' a walkabout, Lugger T. The Hawls be in Ocean 10." She turned to the dog. "You keep him honest, yeah, Lizzie. Not one more stubby or a detour to the Yard."

The dog's alert ears twitched, as if she understood. Lizzie bounded across the pavement and sat at Lugger's side, nudging his hand. Lugger took another long swallow from the XXXX beer bottle and capped it. "Ready?"

Satisfied, Emma climbed behind the wheel on the right side. Sure, I knew they drove on the left side of the road in Australia, but I had no idea that included offroad vehicles.

As if reading my mind, Emma said, "You'll adapt. Every suite includes a two-seater electric vehicle like this one, which allows you full island access, and a skiff to enjoy any of our twenty-six private beaches. The boats have individual animals painted on the bow to avoid confusion. You've been assigned the dolphin boat."

The symbol of love. Russ squeezed my hand.

Emma continued. "In fact, if you happen upon another person on a beach, please take it as your cue to move on. Privacy is paramount at the Cay."

Private beaches. I shared a glance with Russ. I could get used to this.

"There are three restaurants on the island: the gourmet Look Out at the Cay, which is the main resort, our local specialty experience at the Yard, and the Fresh Café at the Pearl Farm. You may also order gourmet hampers for beach adventures or hikes."

"What is the Yard?" I asked. Was it another Australian term?

"Our restaurant located at the vineyard. There is also a tasting room and bar there."

"Is Lugger a regular?" Hard to believe the high-end Cay was on the man's normal route.

Emma smiled. "Yeah. He runs guest charters and delivers cargo. He'll stay put until it gets light and then go on his way. Beer brings on his yarns, and some winners there are."

No missing her sideways glance. "Like the dingo legend?" I asked.

"Eh, fair dinkum. My granny told me and Lugger that one."

"You're related to Lugger?"

My disbelief must have shown, but Emma didn't take offense. "In a way, all northerners are. Lugger hails from the Torres Strait Islands. My great-grandpa settled the Cay in 1905. He ran *The Haven*."

Russ seemed to be in the know, but I shrugged.

Emma smiled. "*The Haven* was a successful pearl lugger and schooner that harvested pearls up in the northern islands. After the Great War, Grandpa introduced pearl farming to the Cay. Our history display is at the Pearl Farm. My sister Meryl's PhD is from Boston University. She'll go on about the legend."

"So, Lugger's map is real?" I asked.

No hiding Emma's grin, even in the twilight. "Lugger likes to exchange a furphy, but Meryl will insist there is always a dollop of truth in any tale."

"A furphy?" I asked.

"Yeah. You yanks would call ir a ridiculous story," Emma explained.

That made sense. "So, there really is a treasure?" Seriously, what was it about me and the lure of treasure? I was at Canine

Cay for a relaxing honeymoon escape. Wasn't that adventure enough?

"Suppose that depends on your definition of treasure." Emma gestured toward the dark sky and a planetarium-worthy dome of twinkling stars.

Turns out I'd given Emma the perfect setup. "Some call the Cay Fantasy Island. We strive to create your dream holiday. Just disconnect and relax. There is treasure to be found on every one of our twenty-six private beaches. Giant clams thrive in fifteen meters of water directly off the sand. A short ride from shore lies the Cod Hole, one of the 'must do' scuba dives in OZ."

No translation necessary. I got that OZ meant Australia. I'd read about the human-sized potato cod in an aquarium of marine life.

Emma added, "I assure you, your experience here will be like no other."

I believed her. I really did. Then why, despite the warmth, did a shiver tingle through my hand as Russ's fingers laced with mine?

CHAPTER 2

Another part growl, part bark, more insistent than the last, pounded through my seriously hungover head. Wait. I'd had no alcohol last night. Where had the brain fog come from? I'd been out cold for nine hours. Impossible. I'd been tired, but I've never slept that soundly.

I shivered at the soft-as-silk feel of the bamboo robe brushing against my skin as I slipped my arm through. My movements felt disconnected, as they had when I'd taken codeine after a root canal. Could that fuzzy fruit thing I'd imbibed at dinner be in the poppy family? I grabbed my phone from the charging station as I stumbled toward the sliding-glass veranda door, trying to piece together last night's events.

The Canine Cay Resort had lived up to Emma's hype. Although not an over-water Tahitian hut, the waterfront suite was canopied by leafy acacias and a small well-branched tree I didn't recognize. The building's carved wood and etched-glass door promised a traditional island feel with a comfortably modern flair. I loved the sand-washed colonial-style furnishings accented with ocean decor that directed your view to the expansive veranda, fronting a tranquil bay framed by swaying palms. If the idyllic view of colorful docks and rocking moored boats wasn't soothing enough, the rhythmic sound of the lapping waves lulled me into a never-felt-before peace.

Russ wrapped me in a hug and whispered, "This is beautiful."

An understatement, for sure. I stood taking it all in for a good few minutes before the exotic fruit basket overflowing with a pinkish pineapple, baby bananas, and unrecognizable treats drew my interest.

Russ and I gathered around. My stomach growled as I fingered the identification card. Seriously, without it, I never would've touched the hairy green thing the size of a kumquat or identified the yellow pawpaw. After a tasty sampling adventure, the local *lobbies* Emma had invited us to try called to me.

Russ chuckled as I commented how I was starving. My waistline told just how much I loved culinary delicacies. Besides, I was on vacation. No dieting required.

He quickly changed into shorts and a polo shirt and waited for me to rummage through my suitcase for a tiger-striped sundress and sandals better suited to the humid, tropical climate. Hand in hand, we followed the tiki lights along the moonlit shore bordered by swaying palm fronds. Decorated with expressive native carvings and expansive views of the Coral Sea, tonight the open-veranda restaurant's ambience included a rash of twinkling stars.

A tall, lanky, twenty-something man with a sun-kissed surfer's hairdo met us at the orchid wall entrance and offered us two martini glasses. "Good night, Mr. and Mrs. Hawl. I am Theodore Andrew Downs, Tad to me mates. I'm your get'cha.

Whatever you need, I get'cha." He offered us each a glass. "Ma swears the Cuddle will set you up."

I couldn't help but be drawn to the affable young man. Besides, I could use all the help I could get to stay awake. I tried a tentative sip. Familiarity tugged at my taste buds. "What is this?"

Given the unique area fruits, the bubbly pale-pink concoction could be anything. Was the hint of magnolia part of the drink's profile or just a result of the perfumed flowers dotting the property?

"Nah. It's made from muddled rambutan and island sparkling water." Tad read my confusion. "That hairy fruit in your local welcome basket is a rambutan. It's in the lychee family."

Lychee. Yum. Just touching that crazy, fuzzy fruit had given me the creeps. Never mind actually tasting...

"The fruit is native to Southeast Asia," Tad added. "Some Northern Territory growers commercialized it twenty years back."

Russ drained his beverage in a long swallow. "Excellent. Sure it doesn't have Red Bull in it?"

Tad shook his head. "Just muddled rambutan and sparkling water. Plan's for you to stay alert for a few hours, then hit the sack and sleep like the dead. Not to be awake until a week past Thursday."

Spoken like a fellow light sleeper. I should know. Any little sound awakened me for the night.

Tad led us past large-leafed potted plants to a private alcove that looked out over the moonlit water. Pink-flowered ginger plants interspersed with the lightly scented magnolias and crisscrossed tiki torches separated us from other diners. No kidding about the privacy.

I smiled at Russ as he held my chair for me. If not for the

flickering candlelight around us, I'd think we were alone. Two weeks of this I could get used to.

I couldn't help but decompress further as our international culinary adventure began. I loved the local *lobbies*, followed by the Australian equivalent of a butter lettuce salad and a cheese tray featuring local Awassi sheep cheeses.

Happily satiated, I yawned as we savored simple flat whites, the Australian version of a latte. No chance I'd get a caramel version. Apparently, messing with the Cay's specialty island coffee was not done.

Suddenly, a voice, followed by a well-coiffed white-blonde head, popped through the banana leaves. "Hi. I am Alice Holmes and this is my husband, Virgil, from Sydney." I understood the woman's charming accent perfectly.

Russ filled the space between me and our resort-dressed visitors with his usual speed. "Russ and Cat from California."

Hearing our names together took a minute of recovery time.

"Americans. I told you, Virgil."

I couldn't see her husband, but from his grunt, I figured Alice to be the social one.

"From northern or southern?" I swear Alice stood on tiptoes and bobbed from side to side to see me over Russ's shoulder. Not that she was short. Russ had puffed up in protection mode. Why he felt the need to shield me from this conservatively dressed, middle-aged couple baffled me.

"Southern California. Closer to San Diego." Russ, cagey? Was coming from Barkview a secret?

"Apologies for the intrusion. We holiday at the Cay annually. Three days here, and I start talking to Virgil's birds," Alice said.

"You give 'em a scare, m'dear." The man readjusted his wire-rimmed glasses.

Russ relented. "Join us?"

"We gather after dinner beachside." Alice gestured toward six Adirondack chairs surrounded by tiki torches on the beach.

In Barkview, the coastal clouds would encourage a blazing firepit. Here, the balmy night breeze invited a cold drink. "We will be down shortly," Russ replied.

We shared a glance as the tropical greenery closed behind Alice and Virgil. "That was interesting," Russ said.

No kidding. Although three days on a special island like this with Russ sounded like heaven to me now, I suppose after years of marriage there could be too much together time. "Do you want to meet them?"

"Up to you."

My heart skipped a beat as his warm fingers laced with mine. Maybe I wasn't that tired anymore. "Might be nice to get the lay of the land. And we are supposed to stay awake for another couple hours, right?"

"So I've heard." His whisper tickled my ear as we strolled down the stone path.

Our butts had barely brushed the wooden seats when Tad set another round of rambutan spritzers on the table in front of us. Had to love this anticipate-my-every-whim service.

We toasted with Alice and Virgil and another couple from Sydney also celebrating their anniversary.

"The Cay is the perfect escape for Harris and me," insisted Lena, the well-preserved, middle-aged wife. "We honeymooned here fifteen years ago."

"He's an accountant," Alice whispered for my ears only.

I believed her. Harris's thinning white-blond hair and loosely fitting plaid shirt didn't scream bodybuilder.

"Most couples return," Alice said for all to hear. She raised her champagne flute. "Who can resist counting osprey?"

Russ's breath tickled my ear. "September is springtime down under."

I knew that. I appreciated the reminder, though, as my short-lived second wind lost strength. "You're an ornithologist?" In addition to being in an underwater paradise, the island was also a bird sanctuary?

"Hobbyist," Virgil replied. "I teach biology."

Alice piped up. "You are too modest. You're a professor and the next dean of sciences."

"It's not official yet." Virgil seemed to shrink versus shine.

Odd. I turned to Harris. "Are you also a birdwatcher?"

"Yeah. My son requested a photo of an eagle inflight." His smile said a lot about his commitment to the task.

"Did you bring your children?" I asked.

"Absolutely not. This is an adult retreat," Alice insisted. "Though the music from that Cliff Villa makes me wonder who's hiding there."

Lena's lips formed a perfect line. "Rap is not music."

Russ and I bit back smiles. Our biggest couple issue had always been music. While Russ's preferences were varied, I preferred country.

"Bosh. Stowaways on the island hardly seem likely. The flight options are far too limited," Virgil said.

I glanced at the expansive darkness. Flights above, but a boat...

"The villa guests arrived on a private charter," Alice replied.

"Suggesting someone wanting privacy," Virgil remarked drily.

Not that nosey-neighbor Alice would take notice. "No one has seen them. They even brought a private chef with them."

That was a shame. The Cay's chef was amazing.

"Lugger turned down their charter. Reckoned they were a

bit dodgy." Harris's smug comment made me wonder how well he knew Lugger.

Russ's cough about made me spill what remained of my drink. "What did he mean by dodgy?" he asked.

"Lugger delivered gardening supplies to them a few days ago."

At a resort? Now that was odd. "Like shovels?"

Harris smiled. "Yeah. We traded a few stubbies last night at the Yard."

"Could they be after the treasure?" I asked.

"They haven't left the villa," Alice said.

Virgil readjusted his glasses. "I tried my hand with the map last year." He pointed to Harris. "We both did."

Despite my fatigue, my interest grew. "Did you find it?"

Harris patted his wife's hand. "We found our treasure."

Lena's strained smile said otherwise, or at least I thought it did, but a rug-pulled-from-beneath-me exhaustion swamped me. Russ seemed unaffected, while my eyelids felt like lead and my mind wandered. I remembered him taking my hand and bidding both couples good night. I guess he tucked me into bed not much later. I thought I heard him slide open the veranda door, or had that been a dream? The unlocked veranda door in the morning confirmed that I hadn't dreamed it. That made no sense. Why would my security-conscious new husband leave the suite and not lock the door? Unless I'd been snoring, and he'd decided to sleep on the outdoor daybed under the palms. Embarrassing but possible, considering my cotton-dry lips and throat.

I took a long swallow of water as I pulled open the curtains. Momentarily blinded as sunlight flooded the room, it took a minute to realize that not even a wrinkle marred the daybed linens. Russ hadn't been lounging out here.

Another bark reverberated in my head. This had to stop. I

shaded my eyes as I stepped onto the sand. The warm tropical air blast didn't stop my head from pounding. Nor did the sight of Russ's familiar blue shirt leaning over a prone body in the sand. It had to be Lugger. Why else would Lizzie be barking and pacing back and forth like a caged tiger?

Never good in an emergency, I just stood there frozen in place. Was that blood on Russ's arm? More important, why was he holding the proverbial smoking gun?

"Stay back, Cat." Russ's warning penetrated my shock. He'd placed the gun on the sand beside the body. Too bad his fingerprints were already all over it.

I screamed a scream I really wished I could take back. A scant second later, people emerged from behind every flowering shrub—all potential witnesses for the prosecution. Alice and Lena huddled together, both wearing the same logoed Cay robe that I'd donned. Virgil and Harris stood beside them, dressed in hiking shorts and long-sleeved shirts with vented outback hats.

Forget the audience. Russ needed help. "What happened?" I asked, barely above a whisper.

"I don't know. Lizzie's barking woke me up." He licked his lips. "This is not jet lag. I feel like I've been drugged."

"You and me both."

His frown didn't quell my concern any. Drugged? Why? We'd hadn't even been here for twenty-four hours. "Is he...?"

"Yes. Shot at close range." Russ's ultra-calmness worked for me. Everything would be okay. I exhaled in a rush, only then realizing I'd been holding my breath.

"We don't have a lot of time. Call the chief," Russ said.

"Uncle G?" I couldn't have heard him right. How could Barkview's police chief possibly help in this situation in Australia? Although I called the chief of police "Uncle," he was not a true blood relation, but rather my Aunt Char's second husband's brother-in-law. Not that the title helped me any—my citations still mounted. "Won't your FBI contacts be better?"

He ignored me. "Tell him everything you remember since meeting Lugger. Look into Alice, Virgil, Lena, and Harris. Something doesn't feel right about them." Russ pointed to my phone. "Take as many pictures as you can before the Australian CSI team gets here."

I loosened my death grip on the case, glad I'd grabbed it as I stumbled outside. "They can't possibly think you would... I mean, you only met Lugger yesterday."

The grim line of Russ's jaw scared me.

"Lugger and I worked together a long time ago," he admitted solemnly.

Oh no. I'd sensed the familiarity. I knew better than to dismiss my intuition. "When?"

Russ motioned me to silence as Emma arrived, dressed in neat white shorts and a crisp long-sleeved outback shirt, accompanied by a tall, dark-haired man also wearing white shorts. The captain's hat atop his head explained his role.

Emma's gasp sounded more like a croak. "Is he...?" She turned away, burying her face in the man's shoulder. "Fin."

"Everyone back. Come along to coffee." Although his nomenclature spoke of years in Australia, I recognized his distinctive Midwestern accent. This had to be Emma's husband, Fin.

"Our local park ranger is on his way. He will be in charge until the constables arrive from Cairns. Please gather in the Look Out." His air of authority brooked no disobedience.

"Mr. and Mrs. Hawl, please remain where you are," Emma added. "This is quite irregular."

No kidding. With Emma and Fin occupied directing the other guests, I quickly took the pictures Russ had requested.

Five scant minutes later, a cloud of dust and the sound of crunching gravel announced the park ranger's arrival, even before the military-style vehicle emerged from the tropical foliage like a scene from a jungle war movie. Just how close was the ranger station?

I needed to take notes for future analysis. Automatically, I patted the robe for Post-its. It's true: Art Fry, the inventor of those colorful sticky notes, was my hero. No amount of technology will ever replace my visual need for reminders, especially with a puzzle to solve. No pad or pen today, but my fuzz-challenged brain still needed to function.

A man whose stoutness challenged the buttons on his short-sleeved tan shirt with a Queensland Parks and Wildlife patch and shorts exploded from the vehicle, flanked by a thickly muscled and equally grim-faced English Bulldog. Their matching expressions gave credence to my theory that masters choose physically similar canine companions.

"Thank you for coming so quickly, Rog." Emma looked about ready to faint. In her shoes, I would too. Murder at an exclusive resort didn't exactly line up stellar reviews.

The ranger approached. "I rang Wolfe. He be inbound." After a quick situation analysis, the ranger freed his handgun's safety loop. This did not bode well. "You there, on your knees."

Russ motioned Lizzie to my side and obeyed the command. The man fumbled with his handcuffs as he restrained Russ's wrists.

"Although my fingerprints are on the gun, forensics will prove I did not shoot Lugger." Russ gestured toward the gun.

No reason to doubt Russ's statement. The man worked with criminal investigations often enough to know. Odd that I hadn't heard the gunshot, considering the caliber and closeness to our suite. Not to mention there wasn't a lot of blood.

Had Lugger been shot elsewhere? But why move the body outside our suite?

Still, I exhaled in a rush. Although I would never doubt Russ's innocence, this evidence should exonerate him.

Rog's arched brow bothered me. "You're a copper?"

"FBI consultant. My wife can get my ID," Russ replied.

"You know what you're about." Rog's growl voiced no professional courtesy.

Not exactly the response I'd hoped for. Or Russ either. I pulled the breeze-rustled edges of the robe together. The pressure of Lizzie's solid body resting against my leg helped keep me focused.

The ranger leaned against a palm. "No one moves until the SOCO arrives."

"SOCO?" I asked.

"Scenes of crime officer. Like your CSI Las Vegas," Emma quickly added.

"I see. How long will that be?" I shifted from foot to foot. "I really need to, uh, use the bathroom."

"As long as it takes." Rog's crossed arms said it all. No one was going anywhere until reinforcements arrived. Meaning: this didn't look good for Russ.

CHAPTER 3

Two police helicopters arrived a half hour later, one landing on the nearby beach, while the other banked toward the airstrip. I should've felt relief, but the unfamiliar blue uniforms and blue hats with checkered bands reminded me that we weren't in the US. They were, if possible, even less sympathetic than Rog, especially after the SOCO investigative team started gathering evidence. Sure, it looked bad for Russ, but why did they refuse to listen to reason? Of course, ballistics would need to confirm the murder weapon and only a gunshot residue test could prove Russ wasn't the shooter, but take him away in cuffs? What about professional courtesy? The man was associated with the FBI.

Within the hour, Russ boarded the Cairns-bound chopper for further interrogation. I tried hard to forget Hollywood images of Guantanamo Bay. Australia was a civilized, law-abiding country, right?

They must've known about Russ's past with Lugger. Why else would the officers only take my statement and leave me behind? When they refused to allow me to fly with them to

Cairns to hire a solicitor, I had Russ to thank for convincing them that I wasn't involved. His parting words pretty much summed up why.

"Find out who did this. I owe Lugger."

"What do you owe him?" I asked.

"My life." He kissed me softly.

He was gone before I could get further explanation. Dazed, I watched sand swirl across the beach as the helicopter lifted off with my husband, bound for an unknown police station and operating under the rules of a legal system I couldn't begin to navigate. Talk about stupefied.

Lizzie's nudge snapped me out of it. I knew what I needed to do. I dialed Uncle G the moment I entered our suite and closed the glass door. My heart rate calmed at the sound of his familiar baritone voice. "It's your honeymoon. What can possibly be so important?"

Words stuck in my throat. His feigned annoyance didn't bother me. I just didn't know where to begin.

My silence must've gotten to him. "Are you there, Cat? What's wrong?"

"Everything!" I blurted it all out in a rush, hardly knowing if I made any sense. Surprisingly, Uncle G listened, saying nothing until I paused for a breath.

"Let me get this straight. Russ is in custody at the Cairns police station?" Uncle G asked.

"Yes. I can't get a flight there until late tomorrow. I can't leave him there alone." Tears threatened my composure. This really couldn't be happening.

"Buck up, Cat. Your husband is a big boy who can take care of himself. The burden of proof is different in Australia. Get used to it. He'll be there until we can clear him. I have some friends."

Of course he did. A narrow ray of hope stirred.

"I'll get him a solicitor. Stay where you are and investigate. Track Lugger's actions since your arrival on the island. The police think they have their man. They aren't looking for the real killer."

That he believed in Russ warmed me. "Russ told me he knew Lugger."

Uncle G's silence confirmed my worst fears. He'd known too. "Tell me," I demanded. "I need to know."

"I guess you do. For the record, Russ wanted to tell you. I talked him out of it. Russ never thought this would come back up. He just wanted to put his past behind him."

Or had he? I squelched that less-than-loyal thought. Any wonder I hated secrets? "Pasts never remain hidden." My dangerous past had nearly killed my Aunt Char. My heart still raced every time I thought about how close that revenge plot had come to succeeding.

"You know Russ's niece was kidnapped?" Uncle G asked.

"Yes." A topic Russ never talked about. Not that I blamed him. "He left the FBI and started his company because of it."

"Lugger was involved in the investigation," Uncle G said.

"Lugger was a cop?" Never saw that one coming.

"Yeah. He was the local constable the FBI contacted to decipher evidence."

A chill shimmied down my spine. "What kind of evidence?"

"A DNA profile. The evidence led Russ to a Torres Strait Islander."

The pieces started to fall into place.

"Lugger arrested Russ before he could confront the suspect," Uncle G explained.

OMG! "The man got away?" Why did Russ say Lugger had saved his life?

"No. The suspect was found dead a few days later. Lugger

26

arrested Russ on some charge. His being in prison likely saved him from..."

From cornering a dangerous man? Or seeking revenge? I didn't want to know.

"Suffice to say, Lugger saved Russ's soul that day," Uncle G said.

I exhaled. "Did Lugger kill the man?"

"The coroner called the death a suicide. No further investigation ensued. Torres Strait traditions were observed. Lugger escorted Russ to the airport on his release."

So much made sense now. "Was Russ deported?" I asked.

"Nothing that formal. Lugger encouraged him to go home and forget."

Good luck with that. Russ's anger had to have been over the top. Mine would be. Suspecting a man of kidnapping and murder and proving it in court were not the same. "Did Russ send Lizzie to Lugger?"

"Yes. After some time, he realized he owed Lugger."

"I owe him too," I said simply. Finding his killer was only the beginning.

"We all do," Uncle G agreed.

"I take it Lugger told Russ about Canine Cay." It wasn't really a question.

"He did. Lugger insisted Canine Cay would be a new beginning for you both. Russ wanted to begin again with you." Uncle G cleared his throat.

My brain went to romantic mush for a second before reality came back with a vengeance. "Who wanted Lugger dead?"

"Apparently, someone on Canine Cay. Find them."

Uncle G hung up before I could ask how. I flopped onto the lonely bed and buried my head under a pillow. Alone in a foreign country, where I knew no one and barely spoke the language. What a honeymoon!

Lizzie broke up my pity party with a head nudge that flicked my phone to the floor. Her mesmerizing light eyes stared at me unblinking until I picked it up. Uncle G was right. Lugger's killer wasn't getting caught with me hiding out here. I dialed Sandy. A quality researcher, Sandy could dig up background on every island inhabitant.

"Geez, Boss. Everything okay?" I imagined Sandy Wynn, my computer-savvy assistant and mystery-solving buddy, twisting her long, blonde ponytail as she spoke.

"It's not okay, Sandy. Russ has been arrested for murder," I replied. How else did you start this conversation? "I need your help."

I pictured her straightening her slouched shoulders. "What do you need?" No useless questions, just to the point. I liked that about her.

"I need you to dig up as much information as you can on the following people and anything you can get on Lugger T's past." I listed all the people I'd met so far on the Cay.

"Like who would want Lugger dead?" she asked.

Lizzie's bark concurred.

"Lugger's dog?" Sandy asked.

"How did you know?" Sandy really was amazing, but...

"There's a picture of Lizzie on his website. She's a champion disc dog."

"He said she liked to chase Frisbees. I had no idea she was a champion."

"Looks like she'll catch about anything," Sandy replied.

"I'd settle for Lugger's killer," I said.

"She probably knows something. Aussies are really smart. You'll need to figure out what she's telling you."

Great, dog mind reading. Not a top skill. The sound of Sandy tapping on her keyboard did slow down my runaway heart rate.

"Did you know Lugger was a retired police officer?"

Uncle G had said as much. Retired or forced out, I wondered. What price had Lugger paid for helping Russ?

My eyes followed Lizzie, walking from one side of the room to the other. "The dog does like to pace." I could get a headache watching her.

"She's releasing nervous energy," Sandy explained.

I joined her.

"Try to relax. I'll call you when I have something." Sandy hung up before I could thank her.

Good luck with that. I dreaded my next call. My aunt and mentor had enough on her plate running Barkview and covering my position at the TV station. This incident could also affect her bright political career. At the very least, she needed to distance herself from me and Russ. And she deserved to hear it from me. Not secondhand from Uncle G or Sandy. One thing you could count on in Barkview was that secrets rarely remained such. I could see the *Bark View*'s headline now: "Newest Barklay a Murderer." As if we didn't already have enough family skeletons.

I took a deep breath and dialed. Relief washed over me when the call went directly to voicemail. No way was I ready to talk about this with my aunt. My emotions careened like a bumper car between raw fear and anger. Of course, I trusted Russ. I wouldn't have married him otherwise, but his secrets had always bothered me. Call it intuition. Somehow, I'd known one would jump up and bite us. Who'd have thought it would happen seventy-two hours after the wedding? Seriously, that had to be a record.

CHAPTER 4

Tracking Lugger's movements in an unfamiliar place—where should I even start? My hand quivered as I scratched Lizzie's ears. Since Russ had ordered her to my side, the dog stuck to me like superglue. Despite the shedding, her warmth calmed me and helped me to focus.

At the very least, I needed an island map, but a guide would be better. The issue was, who could I trust? Unlike in Barkview, I had no local knowledge or relationships to leverage. With my American husband suspected of murdering what appeared to be a well-liked Australian, forget building camaraderie. A killer lurked on this island.

Dressed in shorts, a white tiger-print blouse, and my comfy pickleball court shoes, I walked along the sandy shore to the Look Out, glad I'd claw-clipped my hair back and skipped the matching scarf. Sweat beaded on my neck, no doubt emphasizing my scar. Not that I cared. The tropical humidity really kicked up the heat index.

Tad met me at the entry, carrying what appeared to be an iced tea garnished with a wedge of that pink pineapple, a silver bowl of water for Lizzie, and an apology. "No worries, Mrs. Hawl, he'll be right." Had to love the way his toned legs filled out his cargo shorts. I shook my head, forcing myself to focus on the pattern dominating the pale Hawaiian shirt that screamed happy-vacation smile. If only I felt so inclined.

"Please call me Cat." The whole "Mrs. Hawl" thing needed to stop. So did the pitying looks from the other Cay guests as Lizzie and I followed him to the table Russ and I had occupied last night. I glanced at the simple diamond eternity band I'd chosen to wear for travel. My name may have changed, but my identity had not.

Tad placed Lizzie's water bowl near the seat beside me. The dog sat right at my feet, so close that her fluffy butt tickled my bare leg. I stroked her silky head. Forget the hair assault; the motion truly calmed me.

"Let's grab ya a feed. Chef prepared a yellow fin tuna and avocado donburi. *Fin's Catcher* reeled in the catch this morning. The prep is Japanese with an Aussie flair." Tad's smile invited confidences.

Me say no to fresh sushi? Never. "That sounds great."

He nodded. "Better than a ham sandwich."

I blinked. No amount of crazy translation worked for that meaning.

Tad chuckled. "No worries. It's good." Cubes bobbed in the iced tea he handed me.

I sipped the rich, fruity flavor that awakened my taste buds. "Did you prepare the rambutan drinks for Russ and me last night?"

Tad nodded. "Yeah. I muddled the fruit. The Yard bottles the sparkling water with lemon myrtle sprigs. It's bonza. I mean popular."

"Did anyone else drink the rambutan drink last night?"

Tad scratched his head. "Nah. Mrs. Holmes takes a pistachio and nutmeg draught with a ciggie nightly before she hits the hay."

"A pistachio drink? Is that an Australian thing?" Almond, coconut, and cashew milk I'd heard of, but pistachio? Not a product stocked in Barkview.

"Nah. She drinks it warm."

"With rum?" That kind of made sense.

"That's a beaut." A smile slipped past Tad's pressed lips. "Lugger fetched it for her."

I got the point. "Did he bring it to her yesterday?" Had to be the contents of the boxes stowed alongside our luggage in the plane.

"Yeah. Mrs. Holmes was mad as a cut snake."

No forgetting that visual. "Why?"

Tad shook his head. Not sure if he knew but wouldn't tell or really had no idea. No worries, I'd ask her myself. Criticism flowed freely around Alice. No doubt she'd respond.

"Did Lugger stay here at the Cay last night?" That might explain how he ended up on the beach outside our suite.

"Nah. Lugger beds down at the airfield. Mostly he flies in and out same-day."

"There's a room in the barn?" That A-frame building we'd seen on arrival hardly looked like long-term accommodations.

"Yeah. The hangar"—he stressed the word—"has two flats. Convenient if you're pissed. Uh, had too many beers, Mrs. Cat."

His blush drew my smile. Australian English did have word variances. Tad added, "He had a flat in Cairns too. Lugger called Thursday Island home."

I smiled. "You liked him, didn't you?"

"Reckon. His stories kept many happy."

Lugger did tell a good story. "Anyone in particular?"

"Mr. White."

Lena's high-powered accountant husband? "He believed him about the treasure?"

Had to love Tad's grin. "Reckon."

"You think the treasure is just a story?" I had to ask, but his look really said it all. How disappointing.

"Lugger could spin a yarn."

"Everyone wants to fantasize about a cache of diamonds." Even I did.

"Yeah. Facts don't add up. Those diamonds were lost two thousand kilometers from here."

Russ had pointed out the same thing. "And during World War II," I added.

"Yeah. Japanese attack loomed back then. No commercial transport existed like today," Tad added.

He had a valid point. The likelihood of anything traveling under those conditions seemed low. Never mind that they were valuable diamonds everyone was looking for. "Do you have a map of the island?"

Tad nodded. "The EV outside your suite's charged. I'll mark Lugger's visits on a map." He glanced over his shoulder before he left. "Zed's sis is a magistrate in Cairns."

Was he helping or warning me? Tad's shy smile encouraged me to believe the former. I returned a smile. I couldn't help myself. I really needed an ally.

The donburi satiated my taste buds. A vision of Russ dining on stale bread and a tin cup of water played back in my mind. I promptly squelched my guilt. I'd find the real murderer; no need to starve in the process. Tad brought me the map at the same time he delivered a lamington, a feathery sponge cake dipped in dark chocolate and dusted in dried coconut. Yummy. Call me a stress eater. At this rate I'd need a new wardrobe to fly home.

I savored the flavor explosion as I studied the five X's Tad

33

had marked in red on the dog-shaped island map. All were located on noted roads that spoked from the airstrip located just about island center. These were only the known stops, I reminded myself, because not one explained how Lugger had ended up in front of my suite.

At least I had a starting point. Lizzie rode shotgun as I navigated the dirt path masquerading as a paved road toward the airport. The off-road tires made perfect sense as I bounced over ruts and rocks. The good news was that driving on the right or left side of the road didn't much matter on what amounted to a one-way road. The smell of tropical flowers replaced saltwater as the daylight showcased Canine Cay's topography. Soft sand beaches bordered by swaying palms and large-leafed tropical plants gave way to a more familiar arid, rocky, Southern California kind of look as I approached the island's northern hills.

Despite last night's late arrival, my first impressions of the airstrip being in a grazing field proved accurate. A handful of black cows loitered around the pavement, their tails shooing insects while they grazed undeterred by our arrival. I parked the EV behind a clump of unfamiliar scrub like shrubs. No sense advertising my poking around until I knew whom I could trust.

Lizzie matched my step as I approached Lugger's airplane, secured by choke blocks in front of the A-frame building. A scattering of long-tailed, prehistoric-looking lizards sunbathed on the concrete, arguably guarding the entry.

I shivered. By no means herpetophobic, I still found the cartoony Geico lizard creepy. Lizzie must've sensed my unease because she darted toward the creatures, barking. The lizards scattered every which way. Note to self: watch where you step in the tall grass.

All clear, I approached the building. No cameras or police tape limiting access barred me from looking around. The lopsided lock on the sliding barn door made it even easier. Had the police left it this way, or someone else?

The dog brushed by me as I slid the screeching, WD-40 advertisement of a door wide open. Two metal luggage carts and a two-seat EV with a cargo bed and the same off-road tires filled the open area. On either side, I noted two doors that had to lead to the apartments Tad had mentioned.

Lizzie solved my which-one-is-it dilemma by jerking me left and ducking her head as she slipped through a doggie door —a narrow door sized for fifty-pound or less types at best. No way was I getting through that door. I tried the doorknob first. Locked.

Ugh! For Russ's sake, I had to try. I sucked in my breath and focused on skinny thoughts as I poked my head and shoulders through the opening. My hips proved more challenging. In fact, even if I had worn a Crisco-soaked nylon bodysuit, entry seemed doubtful. Did I ever miss Sandy. Her gorgeous model's body could've easily made it through.

At least I could see the interior. Supporting myself on my hands, I looked around. The apartment was little more than a bunk room with a single, unmade cot beneath a porthole-size window. Lugger had definitely been here. The loud Hawaiian shirt he'd worn yesterday hung on the chair back in front of the utility sink. No treasure map stuck out of the breast pocket. Had someone stolen it? Or had Lugger put it elsewhere?

If only Lizzie could talk. That she went right for the food bowl beside the chair, her collar clicking against the metal bowl as she crunched the dry kibble, made me think she hadn't eaten this morning. If that was true, then when had Lugger left the room? The temperature of the half-finished beer on the table might be a clue. If I could only reach it.

"G'day! How ya goin'?"

The gruff male voice scared me. So much for stealth. I

banged my head on the doggie door as I backed out. I planned to apologize, but the words stuck in my mouth the moment I saw the towering Aussie wearing a logoed checkered, buttoned shirt with the outback flap on the back, and a tan sun hat that completely shaded his head and neck. What had I stepped into this time? "I, uh..."

"The American." His noncommittal tone told me nothing.

Lizzie solved my now-what dilemma when she darted through the doggie door and launched into the man's arms. That she licked that rugged blondish beard with abandon said a lot. "Aw, Lizzie."

A moment later, the dog wiggled out of his arms and sat at my side. The man's sharp blue eyes locked with mine. I swallowed hard until he extended his hand. "A mate o' Lizzie be a mate o' mine." A bear of a man, his hand engulfed mine in warmth. "I'm Zed."

The man Tad had told me to see at the Yard. I breathed easier. "I'm Cat. Tad said you were a vintner." Better than law enforcement for sure.

"Yeah. Spent ten years in Napa."

Was that why his accent seemed less Australian than Tad's, more familiar?

"What ya lookin' for?"

Honesty seemed best. "I'm tracing Lugger's steps from yesterday. I'm trying to figure out how he ended up in front of my suite this morning."

"Coppers asked the same question," Zed affirmed.

That had to be good news. If they really were investigating, Russ stood a chance. "What did you tell them?"

"Lugger arrived at the Yard around 8 p.m. Stayed until he had one for the road after ten. Saw his light when I called it a day after midnight."

I patted my shorts pockets. No Post-its.

"Ya need somethin'?"

"Paper and a pen."

Zed handed me a pen from his pocket and fetched a pad with the Canine Cay logo from beside the phone nearest the door. I thanked him with a smile. I really preferred sticky Post-its, but desperation called for make-due measures. I scribbled my note. "You sleep here too?" The accommodations seemed spartan for a permanent resident.

"My cottage flooded last week. Should be good next week," he explained.

That made sense. "Did you see or hear anything?"

"Lizzie woke me barking at 6:45."

"Are you sure about the time?" The dog must've sprinted directly to the beach.

"Yeah. My head about cracked. Lizzie wanted out. She finally stopped barking when I moved the box blocking her doggie door."

"Someone barricaded Lizzie inside Lugger's room?" My stomach twinged. That was important.

Zed lifted his hat and jerked his fingers through his tousled blond hair. "Yeah. Or Lugger didna' want her to go with him. That dog has a mind of her own."

No kidding. I glanced at my shadow dog, hovering at my feet, looking too innocent. Where would Lugger go without taking Lizzie?

Zed continued. "When I cleared the box, she took off toward the Cay. No 'See ya later.' Lugger's EV was gone so I went back to bed."

"Lugger parked his vehicle in here too?" My gesture included the entire room.

"Yeah. I parked beside him. Coppers asked where it was too." Zed stared at his EV.

"Was it there when you let Lizzie out?"

He scratched his head and yawned. "I don't remember."

He didn't. I could tell. "Was the barn door open?"

"Must'a been. Lizzie shot right outside. I figured she had to go."

"Is that odd?" I asked.

He seemed to go through the motions of closing the door, remembering. "Yeah. I closed it when I came in."

He seemed so sure. "You didn't hear the EV back up?" That vehicle's screech could've woken the guests at the Cay a mile away.

Zed yawned and shook his head. "Nah. I slept like the dead 'til the coppers banged on the door."

"Feel okay?"

"Yeah. I feel like I was pissed last night."

My intuition twinged. "You didn't drink, did you?" Had he been drugged too?

"Just a taste o' scotch. How did you know?"

"Russ and I felt the same way."

His knit brows said far more than words. Had someone wanted us all out of the way? But how could they have gotten to both Russ and me at the Look Out and Zed at the Yard? And why?

"Who was at the Yard after nine last night?" If this unknown assailant had gotten to Russ and me early...

"Mr. and Mrs. Holmes. Mrs. Holmes was going off on Lugger and left in a hurry. Mr. Holmes left half a stubby on the bar," Zed replied.

That had to be a sight. "Over the pistachio milk?"

"Yeah. Lugger brought a pistachio and almond blend. Mrs. Holmes is allergic to almonds. He didn't know. The carton said pistachio milk."

"He showed you the carton?" I scribbled another note and crushed it into my pocket.

"Mrs. Holmes left it on the bar. She circled the almond in red lipstick," Zed said.

A little dramatic. "What did you do with the milk?" Not that I didn't believe him. I wanted the police to test it for poison.

"Mixed it with a draught of Jameson and Island Sparkling Water. Called it Anole Milk."

"Why?" I asked.

"Short for the green anole or the green lizard. Tad taste-tested it too."

"Tad was at the Yard?" He hadn't told me that.

"Nah. I stopped at his place. We're always looking for more island drinks for our guests."

Like the famous buffalo milk served on Catalina Island in California. Tad had seemed his usual upbeat self earlier. I'd have to ask him if he'd also felt drugged. "Anyone else at the Yard?"

"Rog got into it with Lugger."

Did anyone get along at the Yard? "About what?" But I knew. "The treasure."

"Yeah."

Another flash of intuition hit. Zed knew more. I just needed to keep him talking. "What about the treasure?"

"Rog needs to call it. Can't be a ranger if keeping guests on-trail are a bother to you."

"Rog doesn't believe in the treasure?"

"Rog believes in Rog. He's been the lighthouse ranger since Coop's dad ran the place."

I looked up from my note taking. "Who's Coop?"

"Emma's brother, Cooper. We met in Napa. He runs the winery. He's made island wine growing and bottling possible." Zed's respect came through in his smile.

"I'm looking forward to meeting him." I was. The concept of tropical island wine intrigued me.

Zed checked his watch. "You'll need to talk to Coop about what happened after 10 p.m. I delivered a case to Villa number one. Dinna return 'til after 11."

The secret guests' villa. Hopefully, I asked, "Did you meet the guests?"

"Nah. I rang the bell and left the case at the door."

"You didn't even try to peek?" No way I could have contained my curiosity.

"Nah. I heard music. What you Yanks call country," Zed explained.

"Live?"

"Music videos."

That didn't tell me much about the secret guests. A lot of people liked country music. What made Alice think they were A-listers? "Is their need for privacy unusual?"

He shook his head. "Folks come to the Cay for peace and quiet. We respect that. When I returned to the Yard, Lugger and Rog'd gone."

If Zed had been drugged later, I needed to speak with Coop regarding possible suspects. "How do you make the island sparkling water?"

"Coop does it. Let's get to it. Shiraz tasting this arvo. I mean afternoon." Zed trotted to the lone vehicle. The vehicle's logo matched the one on his shirt. "Wanna drive with me or follow?"

I followed, but not because I needed directions. An island with one road to the vineyard and one out made that pointless. I had something concrete to search for, and I wanted to be ready to detour if I spotted Lugger's EV. Wherever that was had to be the last place Lugger had been.

CHAPTER 5

Not even a phantom glimpse of Lugger's missing vehicle as I followed Zed north toward the part of the island shaped like a dog's head. Here, acacias and windblown grasses replaced swaying palms, mangroves, and lush tropical ferns. While the beach reminded me of Hawaii, the drier, hilly terrain resembled California's Temecula Valley.

There was no question where the hiking trails ended and the vineyard began. Just past a metal arch spelling out "The Vineyard" in elegant script, row after row of terraced grapevines flourished on the hillside. A half mile up the dirt road, a chic two-story ranch house stood alongside a red-and-white-trimmed barn from a Norman Rockwell painting. Although we'd gained barely a thousand feet in elevation, the temperature felt ten degrees cooler. No wonder the grapes did so well here. Full sun beat down on the hillside vines, while the cooler ocean breeze tempered the humidity.

I parked beside Zed in front of the barn and exited the vehicle. I brushed the usual dog hair and what appeared to be sawdust off my knees. Odd, where had I picked up that?

"Coop's in the tasting room." Zed pointed to a carved wood door located behind the restaurant and pressed up against the hillside like a hobbit hole.

"Thank you." I meant it too. Zed had been more friendly and helpful than I'd expected, given the circumstances.

"You're a noice lady. Hope ya suss it out." With a wink, he disappeared into the barn before I could ask for a translation. So much for that common language.

I stared after him, amazed to feel a glimmer of hope. Lizzie led the way to the tasting room, her nose sniffing who knew what. How she always knew exactly what I needed to do concerned me. I knew Aussies were smart, but Lizzie seemed to read my mind. I shook that weird feeling off as we entered the tasting room.

Instant familiarity wrapped around me and for a second I wondered if it had all been a bad dream. Was I really in faraway Australia? From the etched mirrors mounted onto slices of large wine barrels lining the wall behind the bar to the belly-up tables also constructed from recycled barrels scattered about, I swear I'd been in this exact room in Napa. The smell of aged oak furthered the illusion until Coop and his black-and-white Cattle Dog met us inside. The dog butt-sniffed Lizzie, while the man greeted me with a handshake and a genuine smile. At least, it seemed genuine. "G'day, Mrs. Cat. Z says you're inquiring 'bout last night."

The Australian accent made it all real. While his sister, Emma, could be described as short and blonde, Coop stood well over six feet tall and kept his sun-kissed brown hair longish. Only the sparkling blue eyes and easy smile indicated a familial relationship.

"I'm curious who came to the Yard while Zed was out on his delivery last night." Pad and pen ready, I waited as Coop scratched his outdoorsy beard.

"Fin picked up beer for the morning charter."

My pulse jumped. I made a note and crumpled it into my pocket. "What time does the boat go out?"

"Three a.m. Gets them to the fishing grounds to set the lines by first light."

Forget me ever participating in that activity. "Fin was at the resort at 7 a.m." He'd been directing guests after Lugger had been found. Had it just been a short charter, or something more?

"Yeah. I hear that the guest no-showed." Coop shuddered as if he'd received the call personally.

A convenient excuse. "Does that happen often?"

"Enough. Ya need to ask Fin who the guest was," Coop said.

Was I that easy to read? "Did Fin go out anyway? Tad said the tuna at lunch was fresh."

"Reckon he did. The kitchen needed fresh-caught tuna."

I'd sure loved every bite.

Coop glanced at his watch. "Anythin' more?"

Lizzie nudged my hand, reminding me. "Yes. I hear you bottle the island's sparkling soda here."

"Yeah. We bottle enough to satisfy our island's use. I installed a capping line last year. The fizz keeps longer."

Talk about exclusivity. "Where do you store it?"

"In the cave with the wine. Consistent temperature improves the flavor." Spoken like a true master.

"It's really good." I meant it too. Russ would love that they cave-cooled their wine too. More than ever, I wished he was here.

Pride showed in Coop's grin.

"Who has access to the sparkling water supply?" I asked.

His furrowed brow indicated confusion. "Anyone working or visiting the vineyard. We don't lock the production area."

43

Naturally.

"Are you suggesting someone interfered with it?" Coop asked.

"I don't know. Do you have cameras in...?"

"Nah. The Cay offers privacy." The idea clearly shocked him.

No surprise there. No security or cameras meant anyone could've tampered with the water except Alice. Her long nails would make that task impossible. "Is there any truth to the story of Lugger's treasure?"

His frown converted to amusement. "Furphy. Fin hunted for the treasure when he first arrived here with Emma. He dove the old lighthouse lugger wreck. Neva' found a thing."

"Lugger had a wreck named after him?" I asked.

Coop chuckled. "He'd have liked that. A lugger was a pearl-diving boat back in the day. Back in the 1940s a lugger sank off the lighthouse. Records show only Lugger's great-grandfather escaped."

Hence Lugger's map. "What do you think?"

"A fine yarn it is. The treasure on the Cay is here." He touched his heart. "It be connectin' with those you love."

No denying his sincerity. Harris had echoed those sentiments. "You found it here at the winery?"

"Yeah. You will find yours too. Guests return year after year for it."

Not likely unless my husband was cleared of murder. Until then... "Do you know who might want Lugger dead?"

"The real question is, who didn't? Lugger found a way to everyone's bad side at some point." Coop chuckled. "I told the coppers that."

Now that was news, yet the police had still arrested Russ. "I thought Lugger was family." Someone you protected. Were things that different in Australia?

"That he was. We all go back generations in these waters. Some just went in different directions."

My heart raced. Which meant what, exactly? "What direction did Lugger go?"

"He was a copper. Fairer man you'll never meet." Coop sighed. "This island was founded on pearls. My sister, Meryl, can tell you more 'bout that. Pearling ended after World War II. Lugger's family settled on Thursday Island."

"I understand the treasure goes back to World War II."

"So the tale goes." Coop's enthusiasm matched Tad's. They made a pair of disbelievers.

The likelihood of a lost stash of diamonds making its way to an obscure eastern island seemed about as low as a Russian czar's diamond ending up in Barkview. I knew how that turned out. Could someone stash hundreds of small diamonds on a small island and no one find them in eighty years? Did I believe?

"Did Rog believe?" I had to ask.

"Ah, Rog. He's pensioning next year. Slow be his pace 'til then. Nothing murderous about that." Coop's half-laugh suddenly made sense.

Unless Rog intended to fund his retirement with the lugger's treasure—the treasure no one here seemed to believe existed.

"Care for a taster of shiraz? We're tapping barrels this arvo," Coop said.

"How long has it been barreled?"

"Three years. Most shiraz is not aged, but this grape"—He pressed his lips in pure bliss—"bests Barossa Valley."

A true vintner's reserve. Talk about a shiraz-du-jour... If only Russ were here. A vision of him reaching through steel bars about broke my heart. Three stops remained on Lugger's itinerary. Who wanted to experience the best honeymoon spot ever without their husband?

I glanced at my cell phone. No service. Ugh! Uncle G and Sandy's updates could really help. Listen to me craving technology.

I thanked Coop and then drove back to the centrally located airstrip to reconnect with the world. My phone dinged the moment I entered the clearing. Two texts and a voicemail. I read the texts first. Uncle G sent contact information for Russ's solicitor. Sandy attached links to an article about a college scandal involving Virgil Holmes and the website for a high-profile accounting firm named Saccer, Franklin and White. Was Harris far more successful than a boring accountant? That ought to make Alice crazy, given the way she tried to lord it over Lena.

I listened to Aunt Char's message twice. Somehow, just hearing her cheerful voice made everything better. "Running out the door, my dear. Remember, nothing is impossible."

Easy for Aunt Char to say when she wasn't at Canine Cay with her new husband under arrest on the mainland, but I had no time for a pity party. I left a message for Russ's lawyer to call me and turned the EV toward the island's famous Pearl Farm.

I heard the bark almost immediately. It wasn't Lizzie. She sat right beside me, her ears laying back flat. I hadn't imagined it. The dog had heard it too. Without warning, the Aussie leaped out of my EV and darted back toward the airstrip. I jammed on the brakes, skidding in the loose gravel. After the dust cloud cleared, in the rearview mirror I saw another cloud of dust and a familiar hat bouncing down the trail leading toward the lighthouse.

Was Harris birdwatching this late in the day? Long shadows hardly made for ideal conditions. What else could he be doing? Rog wasn't offering lighthouse tours. He'd returned with the police to Cairns and wasn't expected back until tomorrow. My intuition tingled. Something felt off.

Head I-told-you-so high, Lizzie returned to the EV and sat in the passenger seat with her nose pointed in the direction of the retreating vehicle. I quickly turned the vehicle around but waited to follow until the other EV was almost out of sight. This single destination road did make stealthy pursuit more challenging. Fortunately, I found a thicket of an unfamiliar bushy shrub just before I reached the lighthouse and concealed the EV there. I jumped out, my pickleball shoes barely missing a long-tailed something-scary slithering by.

My yelp stuck in my throat as I leaped back into the vehicle. What if I stumbled on a family of attack-prone iguanas? I mean, Australia did have more deadly critters than anywhere else in the world. I gulped as my what-if imagination went wild.

A few minutes ticked by. No reptile army came for me. I glanced at Lizzie, who I swear raised her brow at me—if a dog has a brow, that is. Maybe I was overreacting. Could you blame me? I was clinging to the edge of sanity anyway.

I stilled my runaway heart and refocused. Since I wanted to observe Harris, not confront him, I ordered Lizzie to stay. She shook her fluffy head, her response not exactly building my confidence. I tried staring her down, but the look in those hypnotic blue eyes had agenda written all over it. Now I was losing my mind. Smart as the dog might be, she couldn't strategize and execute a plan. Or could she?

The dog exited the vehicle with purpose. I followed her, tiptoeing beside the Aussie as she picked a path through the brush with admirable precision, not making a sound. Not that anyone could hear us over the roar of the waves striking the rocky cliffs as we crept closer to the clearing.

Afraid she'd confront Harris, I motioned for Lizzie to sit. My request must've fit her plan. She ducked behind a bush, her eyes never leaving her quarry.

Originally built around 1900, the Canine Cay Lighthouse had remained an active tower, according to the island brochure I'd found in my room. Framed in timber, then completed with galvanized iron plates, the tower had been painted white with a red dome. A keeper's cottage, also white with a red roof, stood adjacent. Both structures overlooked the treacherous rocky shore break that had claimed far too many ships.

Harris parked his vehicle near the lookout. He stood there, field glasses in hand, scanning the horizon. Had I been wrong about finding ospreys in the afternoon? A symphony chortled overhead, singing some song only they comprehended. I almost bought it, too, until Harris looked around and then turned toward the keeper's cottage. No knock. His body blocked the door for a scant minute before it opened and he entered.

I held Lizzie's collar, hoping she'd remain quiet as we crouched behind the bush, counting the minutes until Harris emerged carrying what appeared to be a book. I squinted to be sure. I couldn't make out the book's exact title, but I did recognize that crazy, colorful map Lugger had showed us yesterday sticking out of it.

Not a treasure hunter, huh? The real questions were, how had Rog gotten Lugger's map, and how did Harris know where to look for it?

CHAPTER 6

More questions than answers ran through my head as I tailed Harris from the lighthouse back to the resort, where he disappeared into his suite. Short of banging on the door and demanding answers that I'd never get, I needed to gather more information. How did I do that when I needed to watch Harris and the map?

My choices limited, I stashed my vehicle at my suite and crept back through the thick vegetation to Harris's suite. Lizzie stayed a step behind, allowing the thorned branches to scratch my legs until we reached a natural jungle-like grotto. We ducked behind a bushy potted plant to observe.

A peeping Tom I am not. Watching Harris spill half his beer on the map wasn't the problem. That he wiped it with his shirt was. Naturally, I didn't avert my eyes fast enough as he stripped. Ugh! I couldn't unsee that thin, in-need-of-muscles chest.

Half-naked, Harris continued to peruse Lugger's map. I leaned in for a better look.

A long-tailed lizard, green as moss and knobby with a black

ink mark, sauntered across my foot. This was no cute gecko selling car insurance, but a potential prehistoric appendage eater.

I smothered my scream, but my jerk backward disturbed the ferns, drawing Harris's attention. Lizzie saved the day. She darted out of the alcove and barked. Harris shook his head and yawned, then lay down on the bed. Nap time meant he wasn't going anywhere.

Time to find Captain Fin and learn more about the lugger wreck. First, I needed more information on the man. Who to ask? Not knowing the players certainly made hunting for Lugger's killer challenging.

I glanced at my phone but did not dial Sandy; 4 p.m. in Australia translated to midnight in Barkview. I guess the rambutan cocktail had worked. I'd adjusted to the time change. I didn't feel tired in the least. It also meant that no new information would be forthcoming from Sandy or Uncle G for a while.

In step with Lizzie, I confirmed the pad and pen were still in my pocket and headed down the soft-sand beach. *Fin's Caster*, the Cay's deep-sea sportfisher, bobbed against the dock, with no one aboard. I waved to Tad, who was on the beach, assisting the chef loading picnic hampers into four bow-in-the-sand aluminum boats. Sure enough, each boat had an animal painted on the bow.

I sighed. Couldn't help myself. A sunset picnic on a deserted beach with a gourmet dinner—talk about honeymoon-worthy romantic. That image of Russ behind bars kicked up my pace. I had to get him back to Canine Cay.

Lizzie licked her chops and tried to divert me toward the food. I held her back. I was thirsty, and she likely needed water too.

"Cat. Oh, Cat, join us." Alice's high-pitched voice brought

me right back to the present. In the shade beneath a swaying palm, she lorded over a square wooden table, next to Lena and across from a tall, well-manicured, middle-aged woman wearing a flowing floral sundress. A cart bearing individual teapots and a tiered scone and sandwich tray stood within easy reach. An additional teapot and water bowl for Lizzie materialized almost immediately.

Alice gestured for me to sit in the vacant seat. "Holland Blackman, meet Cat from California. Easy to remember; her look is decidedly feline. Poor dear is alone tonight."

Did I detect superiority in Alice's directness?

"I prefer Holly." The woman patted my hand. "Just a bump in a long road, my dear." Her smile shone as brightly as what had to be a four-carat diamond solitaire wedding ring. "One day you shall laugh about this."

I doubted that. I'd never live this **Barklay Jail-a-moon** down back home. Ugh! Granted, every family had its embarrassments, but why did mine have to be on my honeymoon?

Holly's accent intrigued me. It sounded different. "You're not Australian, are you?"

"Excellent ear. I have been in Australia for twenty-plus years now," Holly explained. "My father was in the foreign service. I lived in eleven countries growing up. His last post was Australia."

"I can relate. I was a military brat named for Catalina Island. Supposedly, where I was conceived."

Holly's laugh drew the room's attention. "My sis is named Java. Poor dear started school about the same time Jabba the Hutt aired on the big screen. No doubt I won the name game."

No reason to deny it. Kids could be so critical. Alice cut off further conversation. "You do play mahjongg."

Among the teacups and cream, I noticed the familiar ivory tiles. I nodded, hopefully not as tentatively as I felt. "It's been a few years." In reality, it had been more than a few since Aunt Char had included me in friendly Barkview games. Not that this game appeared friendly. "I don't have a card with me."

The look the three women exchanged made me feel like a lamb bound for the dinner table. Lizzie bumped my calf, as if to give me an excuse. But I needed information. "You play for points?"

No missing Alice's Cheshire cat smile. "Is there another way?"

A small price to pay for information, assuming I'd get what I needed. "Do you play the American, Wright-Patterson, or Hong Kong version?"

"Australian." Lena took pity on me. She reached into her shoulder bag and removed a folded paper. "Forty-four sequences. No flowers or jokers. Quite straightforward."

"Manly League rules," Alice added.

Oh, yeah. Definitely a hustle in the making. I glanced at the mahjongg hand list. Hardly easy, but I was in. More like Wright-Patterson than American mahjongg, it still took me a bit to identify the symbols and remember the rules. Fortunately, luck did play a part in the game. How much worse could mine get?

Lizzie figured worse when she plopped on my foot, pressing her collar against my ankle. I nudged her aside.

Alice drew east and broke the wall a moment after Tad cleared the tea service and brought each of us a goblet of the freshly-tapped shiraz. Holly and I swirled the wine in the glass and tested the bouquet. The light, fruity flavor reminded me of black currants and rambutan. I sipped the wine as I assessed my tiles.

No Charleston tile trading didn't help my hand any. Nor did the unfamiliar Australian patterns. Alice won the first game, scoring high points. Not too surprising, the way Lena and Holly seemed to pass her tiles.

I bit back my outrage, instead focusing on my goals. When Lena broke the second game wall, I said casually, "I thought I saw Harris heading to the lighthouse this afternoon."

Lena toppled a tile stack.

Alice filled the silence. "Impossible. He, like Virgil, naps in the afternoon. They both rise early to optimize bird sightings."

That explained why both men had been dressed when Lugger had been found. "What time did they leave this morning?"

"Before dawn." Lena's steady voice surprised me.

So did the timing. They couldn't have ventured far from the resort to be back by 7 a.m., when we'd found Lugger. Could they have seen something? I needed to speak to both of them. I'd start with Harris. He had something to hide.

"We're taking a sunset cruise tonight," Lena said wistfully. "Just the two of us."

A good opportunity to look for Lugger's map.

Alice scoffed. "We're headin' to the Yard. What a' your plans, Cat?"

I forced a yawn. "I've had a rough day." I had. Who would question my fatigue? I turned to Holly. "Are you staying at the Cay?"

"I suspect my husband and I will go to the Yard." She chuckled. "My never-miss-a-fish husband slept through his call this morning." She tsked. "Too many stubbies last night at the Yard. Now he's annoyed *Fin's Catcher* dives the Code Hole tomorrow."

He'd been the fishing no-show. "You saw Lugger last night?"

"Yeah. He sat with the ranger discussing something at a back table. Zed told 'em to take it outside."

Odd that Zed hadn't told me. "Were they arguing?"

"More like discussing loudly," Holly replied.

"Discussing what?" I racked my tiles.

"Lugger leading on the visitors."

My pulse tripped. "You mean about the map?"

Lena threw a crack dragon. I picked it up to complete a kong. The big dragon hand looked even more promising now.

"Yeah. The ranger wanted the map destroyed."

Had Rog convinced Lugger to give up the map or taken it by force? Even more interesting, how had Harris known, and why did he even want it? By his own admission, he'd already found his treasure with his wife.

I turned to Lena. "Did you and Harris go to the Yard after dinner last night?"

She shook her head. "We retired directly after you."

Although Alice's nod confirmed Lena's statement, that she refused to meet my gaze told another story. What wasn't she telling me? Alice knew it too and blocked my chance to ask. "Rumor's Daisy Fay is staying a' the villa," she said with authority.

Whoever that was. "Is that an Australian celebrity?"

Alice's superior huff got on my nerves. As if I should know. Lena folded her hands in her lap and said nothing. Holly chuckled—another of those big-as-life sounds that drew attention. "Heavens, no. It's a pseudonym." Holly winked at me. "Daisy Fay is F. Scott Fitzgerald's fictional character in *The Great Gatsby*. Whoever is hiding out in the villa does not want to be exposed."

Suddenly the shovels Lugger had delivered to the villa seemed less suspect. The movie had depicted gardens in *The Great Gatsby* as a botanist's dream come true. Could this mystery guest relax by gardening? After all, Aunt Char did her best thinking while repotting orchids in her greenhouse.

My eye went right to the hillside accommodations. Lugger had delivered something up there yesterday. Somehow, I needed to meet that guest.

Tad gave me an idea a moment later. Much to Alice's chagrin, I mahjongged on the second hand. Totally beginners' luck, but a win that sent both Alice and Lena on a mission. The kind that meant they'd play until they fleeced me.

Tad saved me from playing that third game. At least, I think he did. Who else could've thrown a Frisbee right past Lizzie and so far down the beach that the dog, while fetching it, would topple my chair, sending me sprawling?

I took the distraction for the gift it was and escaped. While Alice and Lena insisted on a rematch, Holly's parting words intrigued me. "I like your style, Cat Hawl. You'll find your answers. You may not like them, but you'll find them."

I didn't ask how she knew my full name. I'm sure everyone did after Russ's arrest. I did want to know how she also knew my agenda.

CHAPTER 7

I ran into Fin as I chased Lizzie down the beach. Literally. I have no idea where he came from or where he was going. He just materialized directly in front of me carrying an armload of fishing rods. I hit his thick chest straight on and bounced off, while the rods scattered like a tumbled Jenga tower across the sand.

"I am so sorry." I rubbed the shoulder I'd struck him with.

"Ya hurt?" His accent, not quite Australian, but not entirely American either, stilled my racing heart. Familiarity really did calm.

"No," I lied. I was going to feel this collision in the morning. "Let me help you."

"I can handle..." We banged heads reaching for the same rod.

This time I rocked back onto the sand. Lizzie jumped into my lap, licking my face. Ugh!

Fin finished rounding up the rods. "Can I help you with anything?"

"Yes. Coop tells me you found a wreck of an old lugger off the lighthouse."

His brow arched. "Among others. That reef is a maritime safety hazard." I recognized his New England roots as his accent became more pronounced. "The wind and current can easily catch an unaware boater." For a middle-aged man, he sounded a lot like an old salt.

"Did you find the treasure?" Best to be direct.

Fin raked his fingers through his thinning hair. "Like everyone else, I looked, but if there was ever a treasure hidden in the lugger, it went down with the ship." He let the words sink in.

"Could the package have floated toward the Yard?"

"Nah."

No hesitation. "Why?"

"Unlike in the States, here in the Southern Hemisphere currents run south to north."

Which meant a package could've ended up near the Pearl Farm. "Is the treasure real?" I asked.

Fin shook his head. "I don't know. Emma's father used the treasure as a marketing tool. He even developed corporate team-building programs around hunting for it. Established the Cay as a quality destination resort."

I stroked Lizzie's head. She drooled on my foot. Could the entire treasure hunt just be a brilliant marketing move?

Fin read my disappointment. Deploying the usual Canine Cay customer service, he quickly said, "Treasure is in the eye of the beholder. Island lore says that the great dingo spirit protects the secret." He paused for effect. "I've never heard the telltale bark."

I had. At least, I think I had.

"Emma's sister, Meryl, claims she has and that she has a connection. She manages the Pearl Farm."

"What about Lugger?" I asked.

"Sadly, nah. Claimed no dingo ever got the best o' him."

Now that sounded like Lugger. After all the warnings, was it time to disregard the treasure? "Can you take me to the wreck?" Maybe my intuition would sense something.

"Sure. We dive the Cod Hole in the morning."

The famous Great Barrier Reef dive that featured free-swimming, giant, docile cod. I could hardly wait to dive it with Russ.

"There's another guest who has asked to see the wreck too. Happy to run you both out for a single-tank afternoon dive."

"Can I be back before the afternoon flight arrives?" With Russ, I hoped.

Fin nodded. "Meet me at the lighthouse. We'll leave from there."

"Thank you." The Cay did raise the bar on accommodating customer's whims.

"I'm sorry about your husband. Law and order tends to be like the Wild West out here. They'll sort it all out. Rog is…"

"What about Rog?" I asked quickly. My intuition pinged; whatever he'd intended to say seemed important.

Fin chewed his lip, clearly torn between personal and professional integrity. "He isn't as innocent as he claims."

There was more. Hope still soared. The police had taken Rog to Cairns too. I pried for more, but Fin clammed up. With no more information forthcoming, I headed to my suite to organize my thoughts.

Little good it did. I ended up having dinner delivered to the suite. Not because I wanted to hide out, but because I'd spread my notes across the coffee table, staring at them from every angle, arranging and rearranging them for hours. No answers popped up. Not even a good suspect, though Rog remained my even-money culprit.

I really needed Sandy's eye on the evidence. Her amazing ability to research and organize could make all the difference. Too bad the time change made communication so complicated. Even I knew that waking her at 3 a.m. Barkview time to chat wasn't going to net a successful strategy session.

A fancy bottle of the Vineyard's shiraz teased me from my dinner tray. I'd avoided even a sip, focusing instead on the clues. Now...I popped the cork. When my phone rang showing Russ's lawyer's number, my heart about stopped. I took a long swallow before answering.

Russ's signature calm voice relaxed me instantly. "Don't worry about me, Sweetheart. Forensics will come back tomorrow. They won't have enough evidence to hold me."

Why didn't I believe him? Deep down I knew he'd be exonerated eventually, but this setup had been too well thought out —too perfectly executed. "Are you comfortable?"

He must've been drinking something because his snort turned into a real cough. "Remind me to show you a real-life jail cell."

Or not. The vision of a barebones cell in an old TV Western tortured me. I shivered. "I should be there with you. I feel bad living it up at the Cay."

"I need for you to find Lugger's killer," he said.

"It's not easy."

"I know. I chose this destination."

"And it's perfect. Better than perfect, really. The wine is..." I trailed off. Touting what he was missing didn't help. "You couldn't have known."

His hesitation bothered me. "I should've suspected that something could happen. Barkview is going to..."

"Don't remind me. We'll deal with it together. Neither of us can change what has happened." Philosophically, I even believed it.

"My solicitor tells me Rog has lawyered up."

"He should. He had an argument with Lugger last night at the Yard about the map. I don't know how gathering evidence works here, but that map is no longer at Rog's quarters. Harris broke the lock and took it this afternoon."

"You saw him take it?" Had to be Russ's lawyer. Who else would be listening? "Did you try to stop him?"

"No. Lizzie and I saw him." Not that we were reliable sources. "I need to understand why. Last night he made a point of saying that he quit looking for the diamonds and that his real treasure was his wife. Who, I might add, thinks he was taking a nap when the theft occurred. Why he wants to jeopardize his marriage for phantom diamonds is the question."

Russ's voice hushed to a whisper. "Lugger's murder feels personal to me. I don't know if the diamonds are a distraction or a motive."

"Or if they are even real." Popular opinion certainly leaned toward the negative.

"What is your intuition saying?" Russ asked.

"Nothing. Whoever executed this plan did it quickly—too quickly to not have made a mistake. I have to believe if I just look in the right place, I'll find it."

"Or I was in the wrong place at the wrong time," Russ said.

"I know you don't believe that." He couldn't. Not the man who scoffed at coincidence.

"Sometimes. Find out why Lugger was murdered."

"Time's up," Russ's lawyer interrupted again. "Plan is to return him to you by afternoon." She disconnected the call.

Had anything gone as planned this trip? I collapsed onto the bed. Lizzie jumped up beside me and rested her head on my chest. Those startling blue eyes looked right into my heart. I didn't even care that a glob of dog fur swirled around me like a summer drizzle.

Much as I hated to agree with Russ, he was right about one thing. I'd never figure out who killed Lugger until I knew why.

CHAPTER 8

Looking around Harris and Lena's suite proved easier than anticipated. Note to self: bolt the sliding-glass door. One shake, and the standard lock popped. I left Lizzie outside on guard. I had to. If I'd let her in, her hair trail would give us away in a heartbeat.

With my diving gloves on, I rummaged through Harris's nightstand until I found the map hidden beneath a book detailing Australian shipwrecks. This couldn't be a coincidence. Despite his insistence, Harris appeared to be hunting for the treasure. I really needed to keep an eye on him.

I took a picture of the map and the title of the book and got out of there. Getting caught was not an option. My being detained would not help Russ one bit.

I breathed easier once out on the beach and strolling toward the villa. Sure, it was dark, but the Cay's tiki lights did a good job of lighting the beach area, making a play session with Lizzie chock-full of plausible deniability. My plan to meet the privacy-obsessed tenants was simple. It would've worked, too, if I could throw a Frisbee. Seriously, who knew it could be so tricky? I'd played varsity softball in high school and had the jacket packed away somewhere to prove it. While it was more years ago than I'd care to admit, I still remembered how to throw a softball. If only tossing a Frisbee required the same muscle memory as the sidearm skip-rocks-on-the-lake move. Even after numerous attempts, the disc side-rolled with bowling ball precision. Lizzie didn't help my ego any. She tossed her head in you-can't-be-serious contempt and flopped on my feet. Even I knew that the time had come to cry uncle.

We continued walking until we reached a switchback staircase that appeared to lead to an infinity pool on the villa's lower deck. A camera over a security gate ended any hope of an accidental meeting. I glanced up at the sprawling two-story Mediterranean villa more suited for the Amalfi Coast than a small South Seas island. The place seemed larger than the four-bedroom, four-thousand-square-foot home-away-from-home touted in the Cay's brochure. Faint strains of an eclectic mix of American country music emanated from the sprawling outdoor living spaces. Perhaps Alice was right. This could be the perfect hideaway for a popular star and entourage or a setting for a music video. It would explain why they kept late hours. If they did, they could easily have seen exactly how Lugger had ended up on the beach in front of our suite.

I Googled country stars who liked gardening and came up with songs featuring gardens. I also searched for stars obsessed with flowers. Still no luck. How did Sandy always come up with pertinent information?

I really needed answers now. How could I get in there to speak with someone? I continued pacing beside Lizzie, who matched my step.

I pressed the call button before I chickened out. It took two tries before a woman answered. "How may I assist you?"

The accent wasn't Australian. More prim and proper

English. "I'd like to talk to you about Lugger's delivery yesterday." Honesty had to be the best approach.

"The authorities already questioned us."

The investigators had been more thorough than I'd originally thought. Not that I entirely trusted them, with Russ's freedom on the line. "Yes, I know. I just need more information."

"It was a telescope. I do not know the brand."

"There wasn't one there?" The Cay catered to every whim. How could they not encourage stargazing into the amazing nighttime sky?

"Eh. There'd been an accident. The children..."

Alice had said that Canine Cay was for adults only. No wonder the Villa's occupants kept to themselves. Now what? Talking to a voice box hardly helped. I needed to see body language. Her voice said nothing. "Did anyone see Lugger on the beach this morning?"

"Eh, but..."

My intuition tingled. "What did they see?" Even I heard the desperation in my voice.

"One moment." The camera buzzed as it scanned me. "You are not the coppers. You are the lady whose husband murdered Lugger. I have nothing more to say."

My heart plummeted to my toes. Did the police have a witness? If so, it made sense why they held Russ. "Please. I just need to know the truth." Good or bad, I really did.

Russ's release tomorrow suddenly seemed unlikely.

CHAPTER 9

Thanks to Lizzie pressed against the small of my back, I managed to get only a few hours of sleep before my alarm fired. That she'd shed another dog's worth of fur on the soft sheets should've bothered me, but with all the possibilities spinning in my head, I couldn't muster any more frustration. Was I developing a tolerance for dog hair? Housekeeping could clean the room before Russ returned. If he returned. After last night's revelation, I just had a bad feeling—make that a really bad feeling.

I dressed in cat-burglar-black shorts and a T-shirt and checked my phone while I downed two Nespressos from the in-room coffee maker. Not my usual brew, but a caffeine fix nonetheless. Me out of bed before the sun? Not that I wanted to be, but keeping an eye on Harris and Lugger's stolen map meant the man's predawn bird-watching activities needed to be observed. It would be just my luck he'd sleep in this morning. I still needed to be prepared to observe any sunrise activities.

Lizzie sat in the passenger seat beside me, alert and ready

for action while I yawned. I'd parked our electric vehicle behind a shadow of a bush with a direct line of sight to Harris's suite and settled in to wait. I sipped another coffee and listened. No dingo bark, just waves lapping against the shore and an odd nocturnal insect call. At least, that's what I hoped it was. The insanity of the moment struck me. No one in Barkview would believe that I, the anti-morning person with a never-before-nine-a.m. meeting policy, would be on a stakeout before 5 a.m. without verifiable documentation. I'd have taken a picture if the flash wouldn't reveal my hiding place.

Minutes later, Lizzie's ears twitched as a pair of lights broke through the darkness, momentarily blinding me. Virgil's vehicle, I realized, when Harris greeted him a minute later. He tossed a duffle in the back and climbed in.

Was Virgil part of this treasure hunt too? They'd both seemed so nonchalant about the treasure in front of their wives. Were they really birdwatchers?

I waited for the vehicle to make a U-turn before following them past the Villa to a bumpy side trail that cut across the hillside. Using only the light Virgil's headlights put off to guide me, I followed as closely as I dared. Of course, they'd chosen a dirt path that Canine Cay hadn't even deemed important enough to gravel. In fact, dodging branches as the first rays of dawn pierced the relative wilderness became my priority. Heading east made no sense. Lugger's map showed the treasure's location on the west side. With few recognizable landmarks, finding the exact location would be next to impossible. Had Harris seen something else on the map?

I'd texted it to Sandy before leaving my suite. We'd found Skye Barklay's 1920s aircraft by overlaying a 1920s map on a current one. Perhaps a Canine Cay map circa 1940 would offer additional clues. Sandy being seven thousand miles and nineteen time zones away didn't help since she'd electronically overlaid the period maps for me. A big reminder of just how critical understanding techy stuff could be.

I glanced at my phone. A single reception bar on my cell phone explained why I hadn't heard back from her yet. Or she couldn't locate the right map. No. Sandy could find anything. It had to be the connection.

I hung back as far as I dared, following only the bouncing headlights through the woods. Bumping through the bush in the EV felt like a theme park ride. Suddenly, the trail went dark. They must've stopped. I slowed to a crawl, creeping along in the predawn darkness, until a shadow popped up right in front of me. I swerved to the left, barely missing the abandoned vehicle stopped dead center on the trail. Lizzie and I bounced over a scrawny moss-green shrub and hit an acacia's sturdy trunk. Not hard. Just enough to stop our forward momentum.

No damage, I realized in relief as the first rays of dawn peeked through the foliage. How would I explain this? There'd be no maneuvering around that tree trunk without backing up. Ugh! Unless I wanted to alert the entire area with my reverse screech, I was stuck here until the men left.

At least my vehicle was mostly out of sight. I camouflaged it even better by propping a few leafy branches on the back. Lizzie led me down a trail, her nose to the dirt as if she were a trained bloodhound. Who knew Aussies could do that? That dog really was smart—too smart, I realized when she stopped behind a bush.

She'd found Harris and Virgil. Both men stood on an east-facing rock, focused on something in the sky. Long-range binoculars covered half of Virgil's face, while Harris aimed a professional-quality camera in the same direction.

I shaded my eyes into the morning light. In the distance, two large white breasted raptors with contrasting black underwings and wedge-shaped tails soared overhead. The sheer artistry of their dips and banks took my breath away. This had to be the White-Bellied Sea Eagle the men had been so excited about spotting the other evening. No confusing that bird with an American bald eagle. The Australian version had to be three times larger. I took a picture with my phone and made a note to ask Harris for a copy of his photos. This was nature at its best—even worth dragging myself out of bed this morning.

This was no treasure hunt, unless the photo Harris's son had requested was the prize. Was I wrong about the man's intentions? Then why did he steal the map from Rog's home? Call me paranoid. My husband was in jail for a crime he didn't commit.

I motioned Lizzie to turn around. She tossed her head. I pointed back to the EV. The dog shook her head emphatically this time. What was she trying to tell me?

The Aussie didn't like my lack of response. I swear she sighed when I reached for her collar. No secret that I wanted to leave, but Lizzie had another plan. She barked. Not a single, maybe-someone-could-have-missed-it sound, but an exuberant I'm-coming bark as she bolted through the brush, her wagging tail parting the foliage, revealing my crouched position. So much for stealth.

Both men stared right at me. Being caught spying never ended well. Yet the dog barked on.

"Lizzie!" Tail wagging, Lizzie ran to Harris and Virgil's side. Her excited jumping and licks had a more than casual acquaintance feel to them.

"Mrs. Cat, join us." Virgil's voice sounded welcoming.

I stepped into the clearing. "I'm sorry to interrupt."

I yawned as if on cue. No suspicion emanated from either man. Did they have nothing to hide?

"No need for apologies. Lizzie joins us quite often," Harris said.

As if that explained it. "Lizzie follows you out here?"

"Yeah. When Lugger stays—stayed on-island." Virgil's voice cracked. "He joins—joined sometimes."

How close had he been to Lugger? "What is this place?"

"Lugger brought us here." Harris gestured skyward, toward the large birds in flight. "'Tis the most spectacular spot on the island."

To a birdwatcher...

"See the nest?" Virgil scribbled a note in a notebook and handed me his binoculars. I followed his finger as he pointed to an impressive nest made of sticks and lined with leaves.

"Lugger would be pleased," Harris said.

"I don't understand." I didn't. "Was Lugger a birdwatcher?"

"Not in the strict sense," Virgil replied. "He enjoyed sharing Canine Cay's beauty with its visitors."

"It was his mission," Harris said. "Lugar provided us both a map pinpointing this location."

"He gave everyone a map," Virgil said.

"Everyone he liked," Harris added.

Now that I could believe. Lugger had been a character. "What kind of map?"

"A map directing you to your island treasure," Harris replied.

"He directed us both here, and we've developed a mutual love of nature over the years," Virgil explained.

"It is indeed a treasure," Harris inclined his head.

I believed them. Their camaraderie could not be denied. No wonder the men returned here year after year. "Are you telling me that Lugger gave everyone a different map?"

"Yeah." Harris reached into his bag and handed me the

colorful map he'd taken from Rog's quarters—the same map Lugger had in his breast pocket on our flight here. "This one is yours. Rog had no right to take it from Lugger. It was intended for you. This map will lead you to your treasure."

They believed it. I could tell. "Where did you get this?" I couldn't wait to hear this explanation.

The men shared a nervous glance. "Well, Rog took it from Lugger last night after an argument," Virgil said.

"By force?" Could this map be motive?

"Nah. It wasn't like that," Virgil said. "They'd been arguing about..."

"About what?"

"Rog didn't think your husband worthy of receiving a map," Harris explained.

"That doesn't make sense. How did Rog even know about Russ or our arrival?" The trip had been last minute.

"I was with Lugger when he learned you were honey-mooning at the Cay," Harris said. "I asked Lugger where your special place was."

"Me? How could he know? I only met Lugger yesterday."

"Lugger knew." Virgil's confidence convinced me. "He admired your husband. He called your husband 'brother.' He said that was enough."

"Why would Rog care?" I asked.

"Lugger and Rog grew up together," Virgil said.

A piece of the puzzle fell into place. "He's from Thursday Island?" Rog didn't look Melanesian.

"Yeah. Lugger told me that Rog's mother was an islander. His father served in the Australian Navy. Rog grew up on Thursday Island, but he took after his father," Virgil explained. "Lugger never explained why Rog didn't want you to have the map."

"It must've been about when Lugger was a copper. He never discussed that time," Harris added.

Neither did Russ. Two strong men involved in an untenable situation who became brothers. I didn't want to think about it either. Could Lugger's murder truly be a result of what had happened during that time with Russ? The timing seemed so unlikely, but...

I bit my lip. I needed to know more about what Russ and Lugger had shared and what part Rog had played.

CHAPTER 10

If you can believe it, I lost track of time birdwatching until Lizzie nudged me toward our vehicle. Good thing she did too. Who knew birdwatching could be so consuming? In addition to the eagles, Virgil and Harris pointed out a brush cuckoo and a nutmeg mannikin, or spice finch, among many more colorful and exotic birds.

Lizzie and I arrived at the resort with just enough time for me to pack my dive gear and drive to the lighthouse. My stomach growled. No time for lunch. I hated to miss a meal, but...

Fortunately, Tad had anticipated the situation because a cooler filled the EV's passenger seat. In addition to island sparkling water, I split a prosciutto and brie sandwich with Lizzie. I enjoyed the cut pineapple and flaky pastry that melted in my mouth as I drove.

Happy tastebuds made the sting of no responses from Barkview hurt less, but I still felt like the lone survivor adrift on a turbulent sea. Okay, that sounded melodramatic. It was barely dinner time in Barkview. How could everyone be unavailable? Even Uncle G's phone went directly to voicemail.

I parked at the lighthouse's scenic overlook and yoga-breathed. I could find Lugger's killer on my own. I just needed to know more about Lugger and Rog and how Russ fit in with them. Sandy always said information gathering required a good internet connection and specific search criteria.

"Just ask the right questions," I reminded myself. I could do that. I had to. Russ's freedom might well rely on it.

I chewed my lip. No pressure there. Lizzie suddenly licked my cheek, making me jerk back. But it wasn't a slobbery mess, just a kind of wet nudge. I didn't scold her. Her vote of confidence helped. I climbed out of the EV as a gusty wind whipped by.

Fin hadn't been kidding about the conditions. The sound of the waves bashing against the rocks below confirmed it all. No wonder boats hit the reef. Was scuba diving even possible today?

Another EV pulled into the scenic overlook and parked beside me as I retrieved my duffle from the back. I hardly recognized Holly in a black shorty wetsuit folded at her waist, with her hair pulled back in a jaunty ponytail.

"You're the second diver," she said.

I nodded. "I didn't realize you dove." It had never occurred to me to ask, either. The girly, floral sundress she'd worn at mahjongg yesterday had screamed anything but athletic to me. So much for first impressions. Lizzie agreed with me. She'd cocked her head to one side and eyed Holly curiously.

"I have for years. Holidays focused on a husband's fishing addiction forced me to either give in or find something more interesting to do."

Call me a newlywed, but wasn't the point of marriage to do things together? "Why do you want to dive the lugger wreck?"

It was hardly a high-profile Great Barrier Reef dive site unless you hunted for treasure.

"I like diamonds."

Now that I believed. Although she wasn't wearing her magnificent diamond wedding ring, large diamond studs still sparkled on her ears.

"When I heard about the Dakota Diamond mystery, I figured, why not investigate?" Holly sounded flippant.

"Why not?" There was more to it. Was Holly trying to prove something? "What did you find?"

"Well." Holly leaned in to whisper a secret. As if anyone could hear her over the wind and crashing waves, including me. "I looked up the old reports from Broome. The Japanese were advancing in Papau and bombing the Northern Territory in 1942. Invasion seemed imminent. As unlikely as it seems, the only way the diamonds could have gotten out of Broome and come to Canine Cay is via a lugger, and an ambitious one at that."

Her conclusion made a crazy kind of sense. "Fin claims that this lugger was badly damaged and went down fast."

Holly's mischievous smile drew me in. "The better for us to find the diamonds right here and now."

If only it would be that easy. How much diving experience did she have? After eighty years in tropical waters, a wooden wreck would be little more than fittings scattered on the reef. Not a chance we'd find a treasure. Not after so many years. My goal was different. Call me crazy, but I'd hoped to "feel" something. "What do you expect to find?"

"Who knows?" Holly replied. "Ever think about what you'd do with twenty million in diamonds?"

I recognized that fire burning in Holly's sapphire-blue eyes right away. It was the same wild drive I'd seen in every Barkview treasure hunter who'd looked for the Douglas

Diamond. Heck, I'd felt it myself to a degree. Holly wanted the diamonds. The question was, how far would she go to get them?

"I'm just interested in getting my husband back." I expected to be called a buzzkill, not to receive a long, speculative look followed by a short laugh.

"Newlyweds. You'll learn takin' care of yourself is your only chance."

"Only chance at what?" I had to ask.

"Survival." She believed every cynical, unromantic word. I could tell.

Maybe I was honeymoon-naive, but I trusted Russ. Whatever had happened with Lugger would not have changed the honorable man he was inside.

Just as well, Fin's arrival halted my rebuttal. There was no sense in losing her trust. What I did know was if Holly's husband wasn't sleeping with one eye open, he should be.

Fin motioned us to climb into the truck, which was towing an eight-passenger scuba-ready dingy, and we drove down the winding cliffside road to a well-protected, remarkably calm cove nestled on the north side. In fact, boulders seemed to block any ocean exit.

Not even a breeze rustled my hair down there either, but I heard it whistling overhead. Fin launched the boat, and we handed him our gear bags. Lizzie leaped in first. She moved directly to the bow, mimicking an old-time bow figurehead. Fin clipped a life vest on the dog, and then extended his hand to help Holly and me aboard. He started the dive profile.

"Wind's up today. I'll anchor just inside the underwater exit. The visibility's poor today. Watch your gauges as you descend. Hold at eighteen meters. We'll go single file through the exit arch. If the surge is minimal, we will continue. If not, we'll abort for safety reasons. The currents are not to be trifled with here."

"Is it safe?" Was that a break in Holly's resolve?

"If you follow directions."

No argument from me. Too much could go wrong underwater. No sense challenging the elements or a local's knowledge of the seas.

Fin continued. "Sixty meters due west you'll see Lugger's Bommie."

"What is that?" I asked.

"The part of the reef that *The Haven* struck after taking fire from Japanese aircraft that'd just returned from bombing Cairns on July 30,1942. The boat sank in five minutes."

"That was fast. Was it bombed too?" I asked.

"No one knows for sure."

"Any survivors?" Holly asked.

"One," Fin replied.

"A relative of Lugger's?" It really wasn't a question. Fin's smile confirmed Lugger's attachment to Canine Cay.

"Yeah. Lugger's great-grandpa washed up on shore between the Yard and the lighthouse. He was lucky to survive."

"No diamonds?" Holly asked.

"No. He claimed to know nothing about them. If he had them, they were lost in the ocean."

"How did he survive?" Alone in shark-infested waters, slapped around in the dark ocean with no lights to guide him...

"He claimed the great dingo spirit called him home." Fin let that little supernatural factoid sink in before continuing. "The *Haven* was a wooden, gaff sailed schooner. That means it had rectangular sails on two masts, with the taller mast at the rear. It was nine meters in length and three-and-a-half meters wide. It had a shallow draught and a long counter stern. Like the other luggers, the *Haven* had been strengthened to handle frequent beachings from enormous tide changes."

"What can we expect to see?" Better to set expectations now.

"A well-populated bommie..."

"From the wreck." Holly's interruption seemed forced.

"Two metal rigging plates and the ruins of a defensive machine gun," Fin replied.

Sounded like slim pickings. Was I wasting my time? "Is the gun Japanese or Australian?"

"Experts say Japanese." Fin stopped my question with a smile. "Potentially, dropped from the bomber."

"What about the diamonds?" Count on Holly to be focused.

"Be assured any wreck with a treasure sunk in twenty meters has been thoroughly searched over the years. There's no treasure to be found."

Not true. A live reef with colorful, exotic fish and artifacts...

Holly huffed. "Then what's the point?"

"You requested this dive. It's not on our normal circuit," Fin replied. "Feel free to stay behind."

She did. In the end, Fin drove her back to her vehicle. As I waited, I questioned if my time would've been better spent continuing to follow Lugger's footsteps. There was nothing tangible to find here.

Why, then, did I feel a need to challenge the elements out there?

Lizzie's ears twitched at the same time I heard a low bark floating in the wind, drawing me toward the water. The great dingo spirit? What was it telling me?

By the time Fin returned, I'd set up my buoyancy compensator.

"I see you're ready."

I handed him my dive log. His smile broadened as he flipped through the pages. "Sixty dives in two years?"

"Five hundred career. My husband and I discovered..."

"A missing 1920s aircraft." He smiled. "I've read about you both. Looking forward to diving a Coral Sea wreck with you. Didn't intend to scare you. Holly's certification is resort-issued. I dove with her this morning."

"No need to say more." Unexperienced divers scared me too.

Fin turned serious. "What're you looking for on this dive?"

I returned his gravity. "I don't know. All I can tell you is that I'm drawn to the site."

Fin nodded. "Over the years, I've learned that this island has its own voice."

"You have heard it?" I asked.

He nodded. "Every day it brings me home to Emma."

Which explained why a California surfer had turned into a resort activities director.

"Come on. Let's go so you can meet the afternoon flight." Fin pointed the inflatable toward the rocks. "You'll find peace, Mrs. Cat."

I believed him. I just wasn't sure it included Russ.

CHAPTER 11

In the end, I found nothing tangible on the dive, just a sense of the beginning. That the diamonds had at one time been on the island, I believed—sort of. They had woven their way into Canine Cay lore. The question remained, was their current location relevant to freeing Russ?

Hope haloed over me as I drove to the airstrip to meet the afternoon flight. I had not received confirmation that Russ would be on the flight, but the island's spotty cell service could be to blame. Me miss technology?

I arrived at the now cattle-free landing strip as the Beechcraft 1900, a nineteen-passenger, twin-engine turboprop regional airliner, touched down. For a second, I wondered, if Russ and I had arrived on that daily flight instead of hiring Lugger, whether he'd still be alive.

I shook off that thought. Obsessing over what I couldn't change helped no one. Moving forward was my only option. I stroked Lizzie's head, trying hard to ignore her engulfing fur. Russ was safe. He'd be arriving on this airplane, I told myself twenty times before the cabin door opened.

A dog leaped out first. Not any dog, but a prissy Cavalier King Charles whose familiar diamond-studded collar twinkled in the sunlight as she preened on the top step, surveying her kingdom. What was my Aunt Char's dog doing here?

Before my mind put it all together, Renny scurried down the stairs and leaped right into my outstretched arms, licking my cheek and wrapping her paws around my neck in a hug that about toppled me. Not her full body weight, but sheer relief. Where Renny went...

Sure enough, Aunt Char, dressed in chic navy capris and a flowing St. John blouse with her blonde hair pulled back in a humidity-defying knot, stood on the top step with Sandy beside her. Also decked out in capris, Sandy had chosen a practical button-down, likely to protect her shoulders from a bulging backpack. How many computers had she brought with her?

I blinked back tears. Barkview hadn't forgotten me. They'd dropped everything and jumped on the first flight to Australia.

I met the two women at the bottom of the staircase, needing hugs more than words. "You came..."

"Oh, my darling, of course we did. Family first." As usual, Aunt Char's perfumed hug made everything seem okay. "Gregory stayed with Russ in Cairns."

Uncle G was here too? The gravity of the situation hit me squarely. Russ wasn't on the airplane. Nor would he be on one anytime soon.

I hugged Sandy. "Who's running Barkview?" With the mayor and chief of police out of the country...

"Barkview has managed for one hundred and twenty years. Nothing is more important than you and Russ," Aunt Char insisted. "Your mother and stepfather are en route to Thursday Island."

"My mother and the Commander too?" I couldn't have

heard her right. My stepfather commanded the Coast Guard in Hawaii. He did nothing without excruciating planning. We'd only just started talking after a ten-year hiatus. My doing, I'm embarrassed to admit.

"He took emergency leave." Aunt Char patted my arm. "They will uncover whatever occurred there. Never doubt that you are loved, my dear."

No doubt. My mother's remarkable investigative skills had helped me solve my last mystery. "I don't know what to say." Other than "thank you," which wasn't nearly enough.

"Well, I have lots," Sandy showed off a large, old-school black cell phone. "Gotta love this satellite connection. It's way better than cable. I've been gathering the background info you wanted for hours."

"A satellite phone," I repeated dumbly. Why hadn't I thought of that?

"A must on this remote island. Couldn't have the lack of technology hindering your investigation." Aunt Char reached into her shoulder tote bag and handed me another bulky black phone. "Not as stylish as it could be, but effective."

Sandy's sapphire-blue eyes glittered. "We'll solve this, boss. I know it."

We would. I even believed it. I just hoped I wanted the answers. Lizzie believed it too. She bumped my thigh and barked—a remember-me bark I couldn't believe she'd held in check for so long. Before I could introduce her, she went for a Renny-sniff.

Oh, no. The Queen Cavalier's single, behave-yourself *arff* froze the Aussie mid-smell. Lizzie dropped her butt to the ground and sat at attention as the Cavalier walked all the way around her and then offered her paw, as a Catholic cardinal would his ring, for a lick. Lizzie obeyed. No question who reigned alpha here.

"Come. Let's settle into our room and catch up," Aunt Char said.

Emma arrived as if cued. Dressed in another tight-fitting skirt and tailored blouse, she looked calm and efficient. "G'day, Mrs. Barklay, Miss Wynne. Welcome to Canine Cay." She offered us all a water bottle.

I took a long swallow. Wine would be so much better.

"Pardon. I must retrieve our post. We'll go directly to the villa afterward," Emma said.

"Did the Cliffside Villa guests check out?" Despite my best efforts, a bit of panic must've snuck into my tone since both Aunt Char and Sandy gave me funny looks.

"Nah. Your aunt booked our last remainin' villa. It's a three-bedroom with a private pool and a view of the Coral Sea. Quite lovely," Emma added.

No doubt. All of the accommodations were lovely. As usual, Aunt Char had planned for everything. Good thing. Still processing their arrival, I hadn't even given a thought to where they would stay.

Emma directed us to meet her at the six-seat electric vehicle she'd picked up Russ and me in. Had it only been two days ago? My world had turned upside down since then.

Emma returned with a large envelope tucked beneath her arm. Before I climbed in with them, Lizzie jumped into my EV. Oh, yeah. I needed to follow them in my vehicle.

I overheard Emma's question before I started the engine. "How'd ya happen to bring your beautiful Cavalier? Our rules regarding pet importation are quite strict."

Aunt Char smiled. "As luck would have it, Renny has been invited to show at the Brisbane Dog Show of Champions next week."

What? That hadn't been on her calendar. Besides, Aunt Char rarely showed Renny overseas. I caught my aunt's "not-a-word" brow raise and said nothing. She'd managed the impossible again. Who was I to question her methods?

"Quite fortunate," Emma murmured. "The Animal Control quarantine normally lasts for months."

"That is true for pets. Champion show dogs are defined as commercial animals. Like circus animals, they are imported under an ATA Carnet." Aunt Char made a show of covering Renny's ears. "Please don't tell her she is legally defined as property. The poor dear will develop a complex."

"I see." Emma shared my aunt's chuckle while her manager's mind processed a potential pet loophole.

Although Renny remained stoic, she'd heard every word. The dog flashed me her you-owe-me look. This payback would be epic, I just knew it. I smiled anyway. Help mattered far more.

I followed Emma to the Cay's hillside turnoff, past the secretive villa, until we reached another security gate that Emma appeared to open with a simple garage door clicker. The villa Aunt Char had rented faced north, promising phenomenal sunsets. The single-story building, decorated in whimsical shades of blue, had high, tropically decorated ceilings and expansive verandas that showcased the sun-soaked Coral Sea. Colorful native birds fluttered between elaborate balcony bird feeders while dolphins frolicked in the water below, easily observed by a telescope set out all alone, away from artificial lights. I couldn't wait to point it starward this evening.

Emma rushed through her introduction speech, knowing full well that relaxation was not on the plan, and tactfully retreated. She stopped in the doorway and handed me an International FedEx overnight envelope. "This arrived from Cairns. You're due good news."

She meant it too. I thanked her and carried the envelope inside. My stomach flip-flopped as I read the shipper's tag.

"Who is it from?" Aunt Char reclined on a lounge in the shade of an overhang, an ever-so-slight breeze ruffling her blouse. Renny sunned herself on a nearby chair, while Lizzie had curled up at the Cavalier's feet. Fatigue clouded Aunt Char's smile. Of course, she was tired. She'd just traveled for twenty-something hours.

"M-Madame Orr from Dalsia," I replied, shocked the words came out.

"No way. What can Barkview's retired fortune-teller possibly have to say?" To prepare for action, Sandy had set up both computers on the circular teak dining table shaded by an oversized umbrella.

Renny lifted her head and blinked. I had everyone's full attention.

Not good news. I paced as I ripped open the envelope. A single tarot card and a Post-it note fluttered to the ground. The dog card faced up at me. Of course it did. That dang card had been haunting me since I'd visited Madame Orr while hunting for the Douglas Diamond.

"Geez," Sandy said, glancing at the shipping label. "Madame Orr sent this before you left California. I guess she really is a mind reader after all."

No denial from me. Madame Orr may be Russian royalty, but I'd seen her raw fortune-telling talent firsthand when we'd worked together.

"She did loan you her beautiful tiara for your wedding," Aunt Char pointed out.

Getting married wearing a real princess's diamond tiara had been a fairy tale.

"What does the card mean?" Trust Sandy to get us back on point.

I knew, of course. Seeing the card reinforced everything I'd already figured out. "That the great dingo spirit will show me the way."

"A dingo spirit?" Both Sandy and Aunt Char gaped at me.

"So the native Aborigines say. This island is the dingo's final resting place. According to lore, their spirit protects the land."

"Where is the spirit supposed to lead you?" No question Sandy was after the literal interpretation.

"Wherever I'm supposed to go."

"That would make you a dog whisperer?" Sandy's skepticism mirrored my own.

"I know. It doesn't make sense." Nor did the fact that Madame Orr had shown me that card back in Barkview, long before I'd arrived at Canine Cay.

"Perhaps it's not about dogs at all," Aunt Char said. "Christianity celebrates those pure of heart. You, my dear, are the protector of secrets."

Me a protector? My insatiable curiosity made no secret safe around me. Sure, I had a strict code of right and wrong, and I did not reveal secrets better left unsaid, but... "Whatever it means, I've heard the telltale bark."

"A ghost bark?" Sandy crossed her arms.

As if I'd make that up. Me, with zero tolerance for barking dogs. "I know. It's unbelievable."

"Is it a yappy or a big-dog bark?" I search Sandy's frown for a crack in her seriousness.

Not even a hint of a grin. Maybe she really wanted to know. "The big-dog kind, but faint. I have no idea why."

"When did you hear it?" Aunt Char asked.

"Twice. Once when I followed Harris to the lighthouse and he stole the treasure map Rog took from Lugger."

"The one we have now?" Sandy asked.

I nodded.

"When was the second time you heard the bark?" Aunt Char asked.

"The next time I went to the lighthouse to dive the wreck of the pearl-diving boat."

"Both times led you to the lighthouse and were related to the diamonds. Perhaps there is a connection."

I'd come to the same conclusion. Sandy concurred. She started typing on the keyboard.

"Neither visit revealed anything earth-shattering." Or had they? Yes, Rog's relationship with Lugger needed more scrutiny. So did Lugger's connection to the diamonds. Each time I'd heard the dingo bark, I'd been following the footsteps of the bush pilot.

CHAPTER 12

"Then let's get back to reviewing our clues," Sandy said. "I looked into the people you asked about."

I flopped into an overstuffed cushion chair. Sandy's attempt at restraint failed. She had something. I knew for sure when she removed a fresh Post-it pad and a pen from her backpack. "Harris White is not a high-powered accountant. He's a stay-at-home dad. Helena White is the partner at the Sydney accounting firm." Sandy continued, "She's quite accomplished. Graduated at the top of her class from Oxford."

Lena was short for Helena. How had I missed that? Were my people skills that out of sorts? "Yet she bows to Alice Holmes's needling."

Aunt Char's *hmmm* got my attention. "Lena is on vacation. Trust me. Letting someone else make decisions is quite relaxing."

Aunt Char relinquish control? Never! More likely, Lena was working Alice for something. "Tell me about the scandal involving Virgil."

"A coworker accused him of plagiarism," Sandy replied.

"The article under investigation was published ten years ago in an obscure periodical. I understand Virgil denies writing it."

"Seriously?" I asked.

Sandy nodded. "Jennifer's friend called the whole thing a witch hunt. At least that's what I translated it to mean."

"Jennifer?" Barkview's research librarian? She tended to have friends everywhere. It made sense Sandy would turn to her for help.

"Yeah. A librarian friend of Jennifer's."

"Why? Virgil seems to be an absentminded professor."

"He annoyed someone."

Or Alice had. No wonder Virgil had shaken off promotion praise. "Alice bragged he would be the next dean of sciences."

"Not with that investigation hanging over him," Sandy said. "Could his wife not know?"

"Mrs. Nose-in-Everyone's-Business?" The question remained. Why lie? There would be no hiding it when the promotion didn't materialize.

Sandy confirmed Tad and Zed's background information. I added Holly and her husband to the research list.

Sandy typed feverishly on her keyboard. "This is interesting. The only Holland Blackman I've found living in Sydney died in 2019 at the age of eighty-nine."

My heart pounded. "Are you sure?"

"I'll ask Jennifer to confirm. Unless Holly isn't her real name."

Possibly. That Holly's husband had missed a scheduled fishing trip put him at the Cay during Lugger's murder.

A fog seemed to lift around me, allowing me to think more clearly. I'd missed this collaboration. I glanced at Lizzie, pacing in front of the entry. "Why does she do that? She makes me tired just watching her."

"Lizzie's protecting you. Aussies are working dogs. They

need a job. Without one, they can be hyperactive and destructive," Sandy said.

Well, that explained it. The Aussie had been a good partner for me.

"I've visited all of Lugger's stops the day before his murder, except the Pearl Farm," I said. "I haven't met the resident at the villa either. I spoke to a woman with an English accent on the intercom, but I didn't get inside. No one at the resort has seen them, including Alice. Rumor has it the occupants are A-list superstars. According to Alice, they brought a private chef with them. So, they haven't left the villa or mingled with the other guests."

"Canine Cay is renowned for its privacy policy," Aunt Char said.

I frowned. "Did you know about the Cay before Russ suggested our trip here?"

"Goodness, no. Bart Cathaway told me about it."

"Duke Cathaway's owner?" Suddenly, Aunt Char's involvement in an Australian dog show made sense. Bart had been aggressively lobbying to breed Renny with his European champion Cavalier for years. No doubt he'd arranged for Renny's special permission to travel to Australia.

"Yes." Aunt Char's blush confirmed my fears. She'd made a deal to help me.

"The occupants may be important," Sandy announced. "The chief said the Australian police had a witness who puts Russ on the beach during Lugger's murder."

I ran my fingers through my hair. "Has to be someone from the villa. There was no one on the beach when I found Russ."

Aunt Char stood and strolled to the railing. "No one could positively identify Russ from the hillside."

"Except with a telescope," I replied. "Lugger delivered one to the villa the day before his death."

Lizzie nudged my wrist until I noticed my watch. We were running out of time to visit the Pearl Farm. How did she do that? The dog couldn't tell time. Or could she? "Come on, Sandy. We need to head to the Pearl Farm before it closes."

Sandy powered down her computers and packed one into a backpack, ready to go in short order. Aunt Char declined. "Renny and I will pay a visit to our reclusive neighbors."

"You saw the security. You can't just walk past it." Aunt Char's villa had the same entry gate and intercom. Aunt Char's you-doubt-me smile stopped me. "Never mind. I don't want to know." I might not always agree with her methods, but she did deliver.

Lizzie corralled Sandy and me and led us out of the villa. I paused just outside the door to hug Sandy. "Thank you for coming. I know it wasn't easy to get away." No one just up and left a Jack Russell Terrier at home.

Sandy's arms closed tightly around me. "Jack understood. He's staying with your sister."

"At the dorm?" A mountain of chewed shoes and downed curtains flashed through my mind. This was going to cost me big-time.

Sandy giggled. "Relax. Jack is on everyone's radar. More people volunteered to watch him than even I could believe."

I could. Sandy was everyone's bestie and confidante.

"Lani insisted. I didn't have the heart to refuse when your mother wouldn't allow her to come," Sandy said.

Of course, Lani wanted an excuse to miss school.

"It's not what you're thinking. Your sister just wanted to help you."

I exhaled. Okay, maybe I was being a tad harsh. I'd do the same for her.

"You'll never believe the line of people prepared to drop

90

everything to assist you. Your aunt finally needed to insist that someone had to stay behind to run Barkview."

Not that I believed it, but Sandy's optimistic spin made me feel better.

"I'm serious. Don't be surprised if Jennifer ignores your aunt and shows up tomorrow anyway."

Barkview's methodical librarian would change her schedule and leave her Cavaliers behind to help me?

"Chelsea Smythe even showed up at your aunt's house with her bags packed and a passport in hand."

The former mayor's daughter? Her father's campaign for US Congress was in its last few weeks. As his campaign manager, Chelsea could jeopardize the election by leaving now.

"Chelsea is a lawyer," I managed to say.

"She reminded your aunt of that a few times before the chief tasked her with calling her uncle to streamline FBI intervention," Sandy said.

"The FBI is in Australia? I thought they only operated domestically."

"Me too. I guess there really is a branch at the US Consulate in Canberra. That's in the Australian Capital Territory. They are called 'Legats,' or legal attachés. The chief thinks they'll arrive this afternoon to assist with the investigation. Otherwise, I'm positive she'd be here too."

I wanted to believe her. I really did. "This has to be about Russ. Everybody likes him," I managed to say, all choked up. Me important to Barkviewians? Maybe financially. I did get more than my fair share of citations which I promptly paid. Seriously, who got fined for failure to yield to an oncoming Pekingese?

Sandy squeezed my hand. "Stop. It's you, Cat. All the

people you help every day came together. They all want you to have your happily-ever-after."

I sucked in my breath. I needed a minute to get my thoughts together. Imagine that. Me, a non-dog person, had real friends in Barkview? "I'm humbled."

"You should be." Sandy's smile drew mine. "Train wreck that you are, you're the sister I chose. Way better than mine."

Sandy had said it under her breath, but I'd heard her loud and clear. She had a sister? I'd always thought she was an only child, estranged from her parents. My reporter's mind went right for the story. There was one there. I knew it.

Lizzie's nose bumped my thigh. Okay. On top of bossing me around, now that dog was my conscience too? Just how smart was this Aussie? I buried my curiosity. Sandy would tell me when she was good and ready.

Lizzie raced by us and leaped into the EV's front passenger seat. I bit back a smile. The dog knew how to run the show.

So did Sandy. After traveling seven thousand miles, she had no intention of relinquishing her position. Hands on her hips, she motioned for the dog to sit in the back seat. Lizzie shook her head and scooted to one side of the front seat, offering to share. A peace offering?

Sandy crossed her arms. This wasn't going to end well, I realized. Finally, Lizzie glanced at me, then back to Sandy. Recognizing defeat, but not willing to go down without a fight, Lizzie turned on an effective poor-me blue gaze.

Talk about playing the guilt card. No way I could meet the dog's eyes as I climbed into the driver's seat and motioned her to go to the back seat. I'd never live this one down otherwise. Thankfully, Lizzie obeyed. She did drop her head on my shoulder, weighing me down worse than an overloaded briefcase.

"That dog's a little pushy, isn't she?" Sandy brushed long Aussie dog hair off the seat before sliding in.

How do you respond to that? Lizzie had been my partner up until Sandy's arrival. The Aussie's antics had gotten me through the last twenty-four hours since Russ's arrest. Not that I'd admit that aloud.

Blinded by the afternoon sun, I pushed Lizzie's head aside and reached into my dive bag. I retrieved my Barkview Pickleball cap and slipped it on my head. The hat dipped forward, blocking my vision. "This is Russ's hat."

Sandy chuckled. "That happened fast."

"What happened?"

"Mixing stuff up." Her smile teased me.

I started to deny it. We weren't going to be that couple—the one that finished each other's sentences. But the hat thing was all wrong. My intuition came alive. "Russ wore this hat when we flew to the Cay on Lugger's plane. He left it on the coffee table in the suite. There's no way it could accidently have ended up in my dive bag."

Sandy stiffened. "A Barkview hat would be easily identifiable from a distance."

"The hat would have to fit." This was our first real clue.

"That would mean whoever killed Lugger had a smaller head," Sandy added.

"And wanted to frame Russ." I chewed my lip, replaying our arrival at the Cay. "The swap must've happened when Russ and I were at dinner or sometime during the night we arrived."

"Russ would never sleep through someone sneaking into your room."

"I agree, but Russ and I both felt drugged the morning Lugger was killed."

"Drugged?" Sandy whistled.

"Yeah. We only drank a rambutan cocktail that night." It had all seemed so innocent.

"Who else touched your food?" Sandy asked.

"Tad and the kitchen staff. We had drinks with the Holmeses and Harrises on the beach that evening before retiring."

"Holly?" Sandy asked.

"I didn't meet her until after Lugger's murder."

"Doesn't mean that she didn't know you." Sandy exhaled. "Lugger's murder took a whole lot of planning."

"I know." I breathed easier. Not for a second did Sandy consider Russ to blame. "It doesn't make sense. Russ made the reservation forty-eight hours before we arrived."

"Someone has been out to get Lugger for a long time."

No kidding. "I don't know if the diamonds are relevant or not."

"If not the diamonds, then it has to be something from Lugger's past," Sandy said. "That makes your mother's visit to Thursday Island important." Sandy referred to her watch. "They are scheduled to arrive within the hour."

Another spark of hope ignited. That gave my stepfather a few hours to throw around his brass and cause complete havoc. Mom should have information later this evening.

I started the EV and cringed as I backed out of the parking spot beside Aunt Char's. That screech could wake the dead. "Keep a lookout for Lugger's EV. He drove a two-seater with a cargo back. It's been unaccounted for since his murder."

"Really? The island isn't that big," Sandy replied.

Little did she know. "You'd be surprised. There are areas of dense shrubs. The police flew over the island yesterday. I guess they figure it will show up eventually."

"You think if we find the EV, we find where Lugger was murdered?" Sandy asked.

"I don't know. Russ said there wasn't much blood under the body." He had given me critical information, I realized.

"Indicating the body was moved. The police should've put out a BOLO on the EV."

My laugh just slipped out. "There are only four roads and no local police."

"Then they should've kept looking for it until they found it."

No argument from me.

"Good thing the FBI is involved now. Russ is one of them," Sandy said.

"He's a consultant," I had to point out. How far that loyalty would go remained to be seen.

"Tomayto, tomahto. If this is about an FBI case Russ worked on with Lugger, the FBI will be motivated to solve it. Chelsea will make sure of it."

She likely would. I just wondered if knowing the details of a case Russ never talked about would benefit anyone.

Sandy unfolded an island map. "I found a 1930s topographical map that I laid this supposed treasure map over."

My intuition twinged. Was this the missing piece linking everything? "And?"

"I'm not sure. We can stop at the X after the Pearl Farm visit and see. It appears to be along the same trail."

"Keep your eyes open," I said as I drove past the airstrip and turned onto the road leading to the Pearl Farm. Suddenly, Lizzie growled a warning. No doubt she'd heard it too—the telltale bark whispering in the wind. Sandy's oblivious expression didn't bode well. "Did you hear that?" I asked.

Sandy sat at attention beside me. "Hear what? Was it the bark?" No doubt. Just acceptance. Any wonder we got along so well?

I nodded. The lighthouse wasn't my destination this time. The Pearl Farm was.

CHAPTER 13

My vision of the Pearl Farm had bordered on the grandiose. I mean, the world's only supplier of the internationally renowned, luminous, golden Cay Pearls couldn't be housed in two adjoining blue-green, steel-roofed warehouses with tiny windows set high in the walls? The growing area was also ordinary. Only a few dozen green-and-white buoys marked the all-important oyster beds in the turquoise bay located in the island's curve resembling a dog's tail. Talk about controlling supply.

I parked in front of a life-size bronze statue of a hard-hat diver dressed in a traditional helmet, a canvas suit with a steel corselet, and bulky weighted boots. Compared to today's equipment, the old stuff looked downright scary. Any wonder so many pearl divers had lost their lives to the bends, shark attacks, and flawed breathing delivery practices?

Lizzie leaped out of the EV before I completely stopped and sprinted down the dock, barking like a hound on a scent. At what, I had no idea. A lone twenty-or-so-foot open-cockpit work boat that loosely resembled a classic Maine lobster boat bobbed in the calm water.

I cupped my hand over my eyes for a better view of the boat. A dark-haired woman dressed in a black shorty wetsuit bent over a white barrel, her long braid swinging in the breeze.

Lizzie crouched on the dock, stutter-stepping, prepared to jump. Did she plan to swim? A zodiac outfitted for diving was tied to the dock beside her. When Lizzie looked from me to the inflatable dinghy and then out to the boat, I had to wonder if she was trying to tell me how to get out to the bigger boat.

I deferred to Sandy, whose shrug made me feel better. Dog-speak wasn't so easily translated. Before I could decide what to do, the boat's occupant waved us toward the building. Lizzie raised her front paw and then spun around and darted up the shell path, crunching all the way to the blue door, where she nosed her way through a you-had-to-know-it-was-there doggie door.

I shared a look with Sandy. "Barkview down under," I muttered. At least where Lizzie was concerned.

We followed the dog inside.

"G'day, Mrs. Cat and Miss Sandy. Welcome to the Pearl Farm. I'm Meryl." Light-haired like her sister Emma, Meryl was dressed in a polo shirt with a Pearl Farm logo and bulging cargo shorts. She wasn't overweight; in fact, she looked like a triathlete. Whatever filled her pockets held Lizzie's attention. Treats, I realized, when the dog caught something tossed in her direction with a flick of her tongue.

Lizzie ignored the second treat toss. A heartbeat before it hit the tiled floor, the doggie door popped open and a golden fluffball leaped through. Her strides timed perfectly, the dog caught the treat and skidded to a halt at Meryl's feet.

"This is Pearl." Meryl stroked the dog's fluffy head. "Named for our famous pearls."

The dog's golden color did resemble the unique pearls.

"She's a 'Stralyan Cobberdoodle," Meryl explained.

"A what?" Golden Doodle, Labradoodle, even Cavadoodle, but a Cobberdoodle? What was a Cobber dog anyway? I'd never heard of it. The Cobberdoodle looked like a wavy-haired Golden Doodle. I should know. I'd dog-sat for G-paw last summer after finding a killer with his help. This dog was no different. She bounded to my side and looked right at me with intelligent brown eyes. Aww.

"A Cobberdoodle's a purebred Labradoodle recognized by the MDBA since 2013," Meryl explained.

"Master Dog Breeders Association," Sandy added.

I knew that. I'd been around my aunt's show dogs forever. Some things were bound to sink in. I stroked the dog's silky hair. "She's beautiful and so calm."

"She's been bred to be a service dog. Entirely tuned to people who need help the most."

No wonder that the dog came to me for a pet before Sandy. With Russ under arrest, I qualified as a hot mess.

Meryl continued touting the dog's positive traits. "She loves people. Loves the water. Is nonallergic and doesn't require much exercise."

In short, the perfect dog. Well, maybe for me, but not for everybody. I'd learned that after dog-sitting. Every dog had good traits and not-so-good traits. While each dog seemed to be the perfect match for their owners, I wondered if that match existed for me.

Pearl brushed against my bare leg. I scratched her head one last time before the dog walked to Sandy's side for an introduction and shared a sniff with Lizzie.

"Pearl's my best seller," Meryl insisted.

I bet she was. That dog pendant accented with a golden pearl I'd seen on the way in had Barkview written all over it. I needed to send a photo to Ariana, our local jeweler. "Your shop is fantastic," I said.

Meryl's smile promised so much more. "Do come for a visit to the museum. It's unfortunate you'll not meet Lily today." Meryl gestured toward the bay. "She's been with me for going on four years now. It's a shame she returns to the Uni in November." Meryl scratched Lizzie's head. "I know you are disappointed." Meryl met my gaze. "Lizzie and Lily are mates. Drove Lugger looney."

No wonder the dog had announced our arrival.

"Happy to escort you on the museum tour. It impresses most fine jewelry connoisseurs."

I doubted it. Luminescent pearls just didn't sparkle enough for a true diamond fiend like me. At least, I thought so until we passed the early Broome pearling history exhibits and arrived at the Holy Grail of specimens. The display even surpassed Mikimoto's famous Japanese pearl exhibit.

Housed in a ten-by-twenty-foot building and lit by skylights, the showroom presented golden pearls in various shapes and sizes. I'd always thought I preferred the symmetrical ones, until my first glimpse of the knobby, free-form pearls with metallic striations that shimmered like a rainbow in the abundance of natural light. These pieces had to be six inches or more in length.

"Wow!" What else could I say? The color spectrum bounced off the mirrored walls like a kaleidoscope. And I'd thought diamonds were my BFF.

Sandy echoed my wonder. "How can a pearl get that large?"

"It's a clam pearl. Created by one of our giant clams," Meryl explained.

"I've never seen anything like that. How long does it take for the pearl to grow that big?" Sandy asked.

"Fifty years or so. Giant clams weigh an average of a hundred kilos. They live a hundred years or more. Most people think the clams' iridescent mantles should affect the pearls' color. Not true. The pearl nacre is white." Meryl settled into lecture mode, her voice dropping an octave. "Let me be clear. The Cay harvests two pearl varieties. While the clam pearls are unique in size, their color isn't as marketable as our golden South Seas oyster pearls, which are sold worldwide."

I had to agree. The rich, deep golden Cay oyster pearls were eye-catching.

Meryl continued. "Contrary to popular belief, pearls rarely occur when a grain of sand enters an oyster's shell. They are usually formed when an irritant, such as a wayward food particle, becomes trapped in the mollusk. The animal senses the object and coats it with layers of aragonite and conchiolin —the same two materials the animal uses to build its shell."

"I'm guessing that's what the nacre is made of," I said. My gemology classes were paying off now.

"Correct. Also termed mother-of-pearl. The crystalline structure of the nacre reflects light, giving pearls their high luster. In contrast, some pearls have a low-luster surface resembling porcelain."

That explained the Cay Pearls' iridescent colors, running the gamut from shimmering green to icy pink.

"How long does it take for the pearl to form?" Sandy asked.

"Our Cay oyster pearls grow for three or more years. We farm sustainably and don't kill the oysters at harvest. We re-nucleate them up to four times."

"Is that common?" Sandy asked.

"No. The process is time-consuming and expensive. The mollusks don't always produce additional pearls. We'll be nucleating tomorrow morning if you would like to join us. Can always use another set of hands."

"We'd love to." I answered for Sandy too. Her fascination matched mine. "How early?" My I'm-not-a-morning-person mind cringed just waiting for Meryl's reply.

"After brekkie. I'll send word," Meryl said.

"Do you lose the nucleated oysters to predators?"

Trust Sandy to fully engage Meryl's scientist mind. "Sometimes. This island's a haven for octopus, crustaceans, and larger fish."

"What about sharks?" Sandy asked.

"Sharks're common around barrier islands, but they're not oyster predators," Meryl explained. "We suspend the oysters in protective netted pouches where they get optimal nutrients and thrive. The bay is roughly forty meters deep, but the oysters do best at about eighteen meters."

"How did you figure that out?" Detail-oriented Sandy could turn this tour into a PhD class if I didn't step in.

Fortunately, I didn't need to. Meryl credited Lily's excellent research and moved on to another exhibit of uniquely shaped pearls set into jewelry. The two-inch white pearl shaped like Canine Cay framed in gold caught my eye.

"Wow! I would love to host an exhibition of these." I spoke on Aunt Char's behalf, without hesitation. She'd love it.

Meryl only smiled. "The pearls are Cay treasures. They don't leave the island."

The pearls were indeed island treasures, but they still should be shared. Who cared about a stash of what amounted to 1940s industrial-quality diamonds when nature delivered a far more beautiful prize? "Think about it," I said. I wondered what she would say after Aunt Char, the master negotiator, had a word with her.

Meryl's shrug didn't give an inch as she led us back to the gift shop. I forced myself to ignore the jewelry. I'd return with Russ to purchase something memorable.

Right now, I needed information to help bring him back. "Lugger brought you a package the day before he died."

Meryl swayed from foot to foot. "The dear man made a special trip to Brisbane to retrieve the new collection." She gestured toward a glass case featuring Cay Pearls set in a combination of white-gold and gold settings. My eye went right to a breaching whale pendant. It captured the gray whale's movement so accurately I felt as if I watched it live. So much for browsing later. That one was going home with me.

I blinked. "Your goldsmith is in Brisbane?"

"Yeah. Alia's work is quite lifelike." Pride shone in Meryl's blue eyes. "Lugger originally told me time did not permit him to make the trip until next week. Your delay gave him enough time to fly down to Brisbane and back. He normally delivers to the Cay on Wednesdays."

"Lugger delivered here on a regular schedule?" No wonder he had a crash pad on the island.

"Yeah. He delivered the post. Shipped products for us. He especially loved to transport holiday-makers to the island. Gave all his passengers a treasure map to send them to the spot they would most enjoy."

Lugger had certainly accomplished that with Virgil and Harris. "He knew the island that well?"

Her smile and next words confirmed my theory. "Oh, yeah. He spent time here growing up. Always had an affinity to the land."

"He heard the dingo bark?" It wasn't really a question. Would Meryl admit she had?

"Nah. I did. It bothered him that he didn't for a time."

Her wistfulness surprised me. "Is hearing the bark a bad thing?"

"That depends."

"On what?" Now I was scared.

"What you find," Meryl said.

A vision of Russ behind bars flashed before my eyes. I swallowed hard. "Where did it lead you?" I didn't intend to drill her. I just needed answers from someone who'd been there.

"To the answers I sought."

That told me nothing.

Sandy piped in, "Is the treasure real?"

Meryl's half-smile reminded me of both Emma's and Coop's. "More like furphy, but treasure is in the eye of the beholder. This island has something for everyone. My siblings and I are all different, yet we've made our lives here together."

I'd gotten the same practiced, ambiguous answer from all three siblings. Was it remarkable that a marine biologist, a winemaker, and a hotelier could all live in harmony on a small, remote island? What kept them here? It had to be something big.

The question was, what? Of the three family members, Meryl seemed the least likely to spill secrets. I tried another tactic. "Tell me about Lugger. Coop says that you knew him the best."

Meryl motioned for us to follow her out into the warm sunshine. It wasn't a misdirect. At her bidding, we sat at a scrolled café table shaded by a shell-print umbrella. Meryl disappeared inside the building, returning with a silver tray laden with a fancy teapot, teacups with a matching seascape pattern, and a tiered caddy loaded with bite-sized delights.

My stomach rumbled the moment I recognized cucumber sandwiches and rambutan tarts. Yummy. I loved afternoon tea. The Cay's culinary twist just made it better.

Meryl sat beside me. She poured tea into the porcelain cups with practiced ease. "I doubt anyone truly knew Lugger, though I likely understood him best." She methodically stirred milk into her tea. "The Cay soothed his soul. Things he'd done as a soldier and a copper in the name of the law didn't sit quite right. One of them involved your husband. Lugger was excited when your husband told him he was bringing you here. He wanted your visit to be a new beginning for you both."

That she'd used the same words as Uncle G couldn't be a coincidence. "He loved Russ, didn't he?" Emotion touched my words. I couldn't help it. While I didn't entirely understand that brothers-in-arms thing, my life-and-death adventures with Sandy had formed a similar bond between us.

"Like a brother," Meryl agreed.

"Do you know what happened?" I asked.

"No. Lugger never spoke about it. He only said that justice was done. I'm not sure your husband believed that."

I'm not sure he did either. Would Russ have blamed Lugger for thinking otherwise? Much as I didn't want to know the details, I knew I needed to. Hopefully, my mother would gather more specific information.

"What was Lugger's relationship with Rog?" I asked.

"Ah. It's past time Rog returns to the Torres Island Straits." Meryl's scoff confirmed Coop's opinion that Rog needed to retire. "He couldn't harm Lugger, though. They were spirit brothers. To do so would kill himself. Someone else murdered Lugger. Someone with a dark heart."

Now that I believed. "But why?" From what I'd gathered so far, Lugger posed no threat to anyone.

"I wish I knew. Someone has done a convincing job incriminating your husband, though."

Which pointed to revenge. I chewed my lip. For what, exactly, was the real question.

Sandy reached down to the ground and held up what had to be an 8 mm Cay Pearl earring. "This must be yours." She offered it to Meryl.

Meryl reached for her right ear. "Ah. Thank you. I know

better than to wear post earrings on diving days." She pocketed the pearl.

"Have you tried safety backs?" My high-end earrings all had screw backs exactly for that reason.

"Yeah. I will try the lever-back drop earrings."

"But the pearls look lovely on you," I said.

"Emma keeps reminding me to wear them."

"It's all about the marketing," I agreed. It seemed odd that Meryl was uncomfortable with the idea.

We finished our tea and thanked Meryl for her hospitality. Lizzie hesitated when I motioned to her to leave. She looked toward the bay and barked, clearly torn between staying and going. Ultimately, she followed us back to the vehicle. The Aussie didn't even fight for the front seat this time. She leaped into the back.

Sandy climbed into the EV and immediately uplinked her satellite connection and started typing on her keyboard. "The chief texted. Two FBI agents are en route. ETA is"—she glanced at her phone—"thirty minutes."

I exhaled. Why didn't I feel better?

Sandy patted my arm. "Whoever set Russ up left a clue. We just have to find it."

I nodded as she continued to type. "What are you looking for?" I asked.

"Meryl's history. The whale designs are remarkably lifelike."

"As if someone knew the animals' mannerisms?" I agreed.

Sandy nodded. It felt good to be on the same page again. I covered my ears as I backed up the EV. Lizzie groaned and buried her head. Sandy typed on, unaffected.

"Well. This is interesting. Meryl worked for the Australian equivalent of Greenpeace. She published an article on the effects of sonar on whales."

"Why would a woman with a clear passion for protecting whales run a pearl farm on a remote island?" I asked.

"She's hiding something," Sandy said unnecessarily. "Cooper won a DWWA for a shiraz he blended at an Australian vineyard he worked at prior to coming to Canine Cay."

"A Decanter World Wine Award?" Coop would have had his pick of high-profile positions after that. Yet he'd started a vineyard in a less-than-desirable wine-growing area.

"Seems Emma went to the US for college too and interned at a five-star hotel in California. Stayed for three years and then returned to the Cay with Fin. She worked with her parents until their deaths."

"One sister is anchored here and somehow brings her siblings back when their parents pass," I said aloud.

"That about sums it up." Sandy whistled. "I bet they know where the diamonds are."

I agreed. "Or were. They could've used them to build the island into the resort it is today." Not that I blamed them. Finders keepers regarding an eighty-year-old loss.

"Think Lugger knew too?" Sandy asked.

"If he did, he definitely would've been part of that cover-up."

"What if Lugger figured it out and threatened to report them?" Sandy's comment wasn't really a question. "You know, the right circumstances could cause good people to make desperate decisions."

We had seen that firsthand. Coop, Meryl, and Emma murderers? From an investigative perspective, Emma did have access to Russ and my food to drug us. Fin had opportunity. His morning charter's no-show put him at the Cay during the murder. Why frame Russ? That piece didn't fit.

Lugger's murder felt more personal. Revenge kept coming to mind. Revenge for what?

CHAPTER 14

"Let's see where Lugger's map leads us." Sandy unfolded the all-too-familiar paper.

My intuition immediately went on alert. I was getting closer. I could feel it. It even twinged the moment Sandy pointed to a cone-shaped rock I was driving by on the dirt trail. "Turn here. It has to be the turnoff."

My gaze locked on the map she waved in front of me. Distracted, I misjudged the curve and bumped off the narrow path. I swerved to compensate, grabbing the steering wheel for balance. Sandy and Lizzie weren't so lucky. They jerked sideways, bumping into the fiberglass EV's doors. I'm just glad they didn't fall out.

"Geez. Thought you could multitask." Sandy rubbed her abused shoulder. Lizzie sat sphinx-style across the seat, panting.

Where was my head? I muscled the vehicle back onto the path and turned where Sandy directed. If not for fresh tire tracks, I never would've seen the quasi-trail. The thick brush and low-branched acacias scratched the EV's roof and sides as we wove our way through.

"Turn right here," Sandy said.

I obeyed. Well, sort of.

"The other right," Sandy shouted.

Her panic fueled mine. I jammed on the brakes. Too late. The vehicle skidded in the loose gravel and smashed into a thick tree trunk. I winced. The something-broke crunching sound did not bode well.

Quickly, I pressed the reverse button. No screech. Not even an electric hum. I'd really done it this time.

No wishing away this accident. I stepped out from behind the wheel for a better look. The EV tilted. Not enough to tip over, but it sat at a definite angle. The front-end damage didn't look bad. The small dent and scratch appeared to be cosmetic. The rear end was the real story. It wasn't what I'd hit, but rather what I'd run over. The entire vehicle nested atop a thorny bush. Not a big deal. Together, Sandy and I could push it back onto solid ground. Thankfully, I'd worn closed-toe pickleball shoes. That plant looked like it had spikes.

Lizzie flew from the back seat. How she accelerated from sitting to a quality long jump amazed me. Without even an over-the-shoulder look back, the Aussie sprinted down the path Sandy had directed me to follow. I started to follow, but Sandy didn't move.

One look at her stylish flip-flops and I saw the problem. Even with her long legs, she'd never clear the stickers. "Wanna try my shoes?" I asked, only half kidding.

"You're joking."

A Cinderella shoe moment it would not be. I doubted her toes would even fit into my shoes. What other choice did we have? I couldn't just leave her here, stranded.

My eye settled on my dive bag in the back. I had an idea. I

unzipped the duffle bag and dug out my damp neoprene diving booties. Not the most fashionable option, but they would stretch enough to protect her feet.

Sandy thanked me with a smile and quickly squeezed into the ankle-high booties. Together we ran after Lizzie, whose barking seemed louder the closer we got. At least I thought it was Lizzie's barking until I saw the dog, with her head buried beneath her paws, lying in the driver's seat of an abandoned EV—Lugger's EV. I recognized the flatbed from our arrival. We'd found it.

Anticipation tingled through me. Sandy's hand on my wrist stopped my investigation. "Hold it. Don't touch anything," She pulled a pair of light-blue plastic gloves from her shorts pocket. "The chief lectured me on proper procedure all the way from LA."

"That's like fourteen hours," I groaned for her benefit.

"Yeah. I got the message."

So did I. Uncle G was protecting me too. It felt way too good.

"Let me take a few pictures and send them to the chief before we investigate," Sandy said.

I didn't argue. Sandy circled the vehicle, taking pictures with daunting ease. Besides, Lizzie had my full attention. The Aussie barely lifted her head as we approached. A tear slipped down my cheek as her heartfelt yowl echoed around us.

An answering howl stopped me cold. Lizzie, too—she jumped to her feet and trotted to my side. No. I had to have imagined it. In life, Lugger had not thought he'd connected with the dingo spirit. Yet, in death...

Sandy touched my arm. "What just happened?"

I sniffled. "Russ is going to be okay."

"Of course he will." Sandy hugged me so tightly that I gasped for air. "None of us will stop until he is."

I believed her. I also believed someone or something else was watching. "Let's take a look at the vehicle."

Video rolling, we approached Lugger's EV. A bloodstain on the seat caught my eye. I took a picture of the blotch. The FBI could tell us if it was Lugger's blood or not. I peeked beneath the seat. A beer bottle and two candy wrappers hardly qualified as earth-shattering. I removed my plastic gloves. Sandy bagged them as evidence too. Talk about thorough. I started to argue, but a sparkle between the seats caught my eye.

A diamond? Sandy's cough stopped a closer inspection. She filmed the location as I crushed my fingers into another pair of gloves. I knelt on the bucket seat and blindly slipped my hands between the leather upholstery. I felt the stone with my fingertip, but it slipped farther behind the seat. I contorted like a pretzel, reaching even farther. I felt the hard edge again...

Sandy snatched it from the back seat. "It's a diamond." She held the clear stone up to the light, sending rainbow prisms across the flora.

Round, brilliant cut, with good clarity, and roughly half a carat—I couldn't say for sure if it was a natural diamond or cubic zirconia.

"Definitely not one of the missing stones from the 1940s. The cut is too modern," I said.

Sandy nodded. She knew better than to challenge my jewelry knowledge. "Could it have fallen out of a setting?"

I looked closer. "No scratches or nicks." Not that I expected to see any in the hardest substance known to man. "The better question is, how did it get here? Lizzie rode shotgun." And had no diamonds on her utilitarian leather collar.

"We will need to figure that out later. At least we have a clue." Sandy bagged the stone and referred to the map. "If we're finished here, the map's X is that direction."

Lizzie brushed by Sandy to lead us through the trees to a

rocky cliff. Salt air filled my senses as I stared at the Pearl Farm below. Beyond the warehouses, overlooking the bay, I noticed twin whitewashed cottages covered in what looked like trellised climbing frangipani that had to be where Lily and Meryl lived. Nothing elaborate, but what a porch view they had.

Lizzie sat directly in front of a small alcove, her paw resting on a rock pile.

My intuition sparked. So far the dog had been spot-on. I shooed Lizzie aside. The Aussie leaped closer and licked my face. Ugh! I lifted the top rock. Sure enough, a weathered metal cigar-size tube filled the crevice. "Yeah!" I couldn't help my enthusiasm.

Sandy hovered over my shoulder, blocking the light as I pulled it out and twisted off the top. I held my breath as I pulled out a rolled piece of white paper. New paper untouched by age and written in bold, mannish print. This was no clue from the past, but something Lugger had written. I read the words out loud.

Beneath the surface you will find deeper meaning.

"Beneath the surface of what?" Sandy's question echoed my thought exactly.

Water came to mind, but... "The lugger's wreck site was nothing more than sand and scattered debris."

Sandy reread the clue. "It could be referring to water. Are there artifacts from the wreck anywhere else?"

"Holly mentioned an exhibit at the lighthouse. If Lugger intended to leave additional clues there for Russ, it could be how Rog found out about it."

"Is it open?"

"I don't think so. Rog is still in Cairns. Maybe Emma can let us in."

Sandy jumped on my suggestion. She dialed the Cay on the satellite phone and asked to speak to Emma while I looked out over the azure ocean. As if cued, Lizzie slid her head under my hand and leaned into my side. I scratched automatically, drawing comfort from her solid presence. The clues scattered like random pieces to an unsolved puzzle. Not unlike most mysteries I'd worked through, but this time was different. My husband's freedom hung in the balance.

"Emma said she'd meet us at the lighthouse in twenty minutes." Sandy's announcement brought me right back to the present. "What's the deal with 'No worries, mate?' They can't be that accommodating."

"It's the Australian way," I replied with complete confidence. At least here at the Cay. If someone wasn't trying to frame Russ, I'd be in heaven.

"The Old Barkview Inn could take some lessons," Sandy said.

My laugh just slipped out. "Good luck telling Franklin that." Called "the magician," the inn's concierge took customer service to a level five-star pamper palace resorts could only aspire to.

"Do you think Lugger could've been murdered while hiding the clue?" Sandy asked.

"It would explain why his vehicle was here. Not why someone carried him to the beach to frame Russ."

Sandy's frustration echoed mine. We were still missing something important.

We got the EV back on the trail and drove to the lighthouse. This time I didn't hear the telltale bark. Since we arrived at the lighthouse a few moments before Emma, I pointed out where I'd seen Harris break into Rog's quarters to retrieve the map.

"Could he have had a key?" Sandy asked.

"I doubt it. Maybe he's a master lock-pick."

"Maybe an important skill for a stay-at-home man with two precocious young sons," Sandy suggested.

The vision of me banging on a door while mini-Russ giggled at me from the other side about stopped my heart.

"You okay? You look like you've seen a ghost."

"More like a nightmare."

Sandy's smile burst into a grin. "Methinks Auntie Sandy is going to love this."

Was I that easy to read? I must've blushed to my roots. "I'm missing one key ingredient right now."

Emma's arrival interrupted Sandy's response. I figured it was her when Lizzie took off down the path, barking. A minute later, Emma drove up with Lizzie seated beside her in the EV. The warm breeze rustled the dog's fur, but not Emma's. In fact, not even a hair appeared out of place in the many hours since she'd greeted my aunt. I ran my fingers through my locks, limp from humidity. What I wouldn't give for a can of her hairspray.

"G'day. Come along." We matched her hurried stride as we walked to the single white door leading into the lighthouse tower. "It's not much of an exhibit. The sea claimed most of the lugger wreck artifacts before recreational diving came to the Cay. My mother extensively researched the vessel and recreated much of the daily activities in paintings. The lighthouse itself was built in 1905..."

Emma's historical tour, complemented by photographs, paintings, and etchings drawn by Emma's mother herself, really gave a sense of Canine Cay's beginnings and its many struggles to fend off the tax collector.

"The photography is remarkable," Sandy said.

"My mother was a talented photographer. She came to the Cay on a photoshoot and never left." I understood her pensive exhale. I'd lost my dad too.

"Love at first sight?" It was Sandy's turn at wistfulness. There was a happily-ever-after for her too.

"The island spoke to her," Emma said.

"She heard the dingo bark?" I held my concern in check, barely.

"Yeah. Dad thought he should've heard it. I'm not so sure."

"Why?" I asked.

"Only the chosen few hear the bark."

"Why are they chosen?" Sandy asked.

"No one knows."

"You think it should have been you instead of Meryl?" Emma's refusal to meet my eye confirmed everything. Emma, who'd brought the family...

"Yet a total stranger heard the bark," Sandy said. "Why?"

"Legend says that the dingo seeks a new protector when needed." Emma eyed me funny.

"Is Meryl going somewhere?" I asked.

"Her restless spirit would say yes, but she knows where she belongs," Emma replied.

More like, knew her responsibilities. I sucked in my breath. No. No and no. I was an American city girl. Not island material. I refused to fill in.

"How does that dingo spirit thing work?" Trust Sandy to stay on point while my head spun like an out-of-control top.

"Well..." Emma leaned against the wall, settling in for what promised to be a long story. "Since the beginning, the dingo worked as one with man. Generations of men and dogs hunted together and protected their children. On the mainland, the story goes that a woman banished the dingo. The continuous bond broken, the dingo went off on his own. He competed with man for food and shelter until man hunted the dogs.

"Here on the island, that bond never broke. The dingo eventually died off. The last dingo watches over this land to protect both the island's secrets and its charges."

"When was the last dingo here?" Sandy asked.

"Long ago. Since then, though, the dingo spirit speaks through a protector who safeguards both the land and people."

I shared a glance with Sandy. "Is there more than one protector?"

Emma shook her head. "Not that I know of."

Yet I'd heard "the bark." Did that mean Meryl was in danger? I didn't know the dingo's secrets. While curiosity did draw me toward answers, I flat out didn't want to know.

"Is the treasure real?" Sandy asked.

"Furphy. My father created the treasure to save us in the 1980s," Emma explained.

She sounded so convincing. Maybe I just didn't want to believe that there was no treasure.

The artifacts recovered from the wreck didn't contain another clue about the murder. In addition to some metal parts, a small, nonspherical, natural pearl as well as oyster shells were exhibited beside the old-fashioned mother-of-pearl buttons in a glass case.

What had Lugger meant by "beneath the surface?" The family's seemingly cohesive relationship? I even peeked at the underside of Lizzie's collar. Wouldn't be the first time I'd discovered information hidden on a dog's collar. No luck. Either Lugger had been murdered before he'd had time to hide additional clues, or I hadn't figured it out yet.

CHAPTER 15

My mother called as we drove back to the villa Aunt Char had rented. The satellite phone's death-dirge ring about sent my heart into palpitations. Was it a sign?

I pulled to the side of the path and glared at Sandy.

"I'll change it," she promised.

I answered the call. "Hi, Mom. You're on speaker with Sandy and me." Lizzie butted her head into my shoulder and barked, refusing to be left out. "That's Lizzie. She's a really smart Australian Shepherd."

"Goodness. A big, hairy dog." I pictured her just-ate-lemons lip pucker. I pulled an offending dark dog hair off my shorts in agreement.

"How's Thursday Island, Mrs. O?" Sandy handed me Post-its and a pen.

I sat back, ready to take notes.

"Quite interesting." Before I could ask what that meant, she continued, "This is an expensive call, so here's what I've found so far. The perp..."

I loved her cops and robbers reference.

"...was a kidnapper-for-hire. Seriously, who knew they existed. Anyway, this guy worked in Mexico and the US, mostly for the cartels. A vicious way to keep employees in line. The FBI named him the Spirit since he seemed to just vanish when cornered. Russ's niece was his seventh victim and how Russ got involved. As you know, her case didn't end well. The Spirit vanished as per his MO. Dozens of leads led nowhere. Russ refused to quit."

I loved that about him.

"He left the FBI and started looking for the perp on his own." I swallowed hard. That had to have torn him apart. "Is that when he partnered with Blue Diamond Security?" Sandy asked.

"Yes, Russ protects his own. He found DNA from his niece's case that had the markers of a Torres Straits Islander. Unfortunately, there was no identity match on file. Russ came to Thursday Island, where he met Lugger, who was the senior constable at the time. Rumor has it that Lugger immediately knew who the perp was since he'd served with the guy in the Australian Army."

"Why wasn't there DNA in the armed forces database?" Sandy asked.

"That's where this gets interesting. The guy never existed, as far as military records are concerned. Yet I found a picture of him with Lugger T in uniform in the Thursday Island newspaper."

"Great job, Mom." I meant it.

"There's more. The Thursday Island mayor ordered Lugger to bring the guy in alive. Most believe that's why Lugger locked up Russ for obstruction."

So my husband really *was* familiar with Australian prisons.

"Lugger found the guy living lavishly on an outlying island. Lugger offered him a chance to go 'the island way.' Two days later, the perp washed up on a local beach. Coroner labeled the death an accidental drowning."

"He went the island way." No wonder Russ had been angry. Had the end really justified the means here?

"The perp left all of his worldly possessions to the islanders," Mom added.

"A real Robin Hood," Sandy added dryly.

"So it seems. The islanders adore him. The money financed a much-needed new primary school, a sports center, and a medical facility."

"What happened to Lugger?" Although I'd known the story's basics, the details helped.

"The mayor was a mainlander. Name was"—I heard pages turning in the background—"Randall Thornton. Popular opinion is he wanted the press associated with the case. Thornton fired Lugger. Then lost reelection. A colonel"—more pages turned—"named Mathew Morgan buried the perp's military identity. He was court-martialed and dishonorably discharged for it."

Talk about coincidences. Not.

"The Commander and I believe there's more to the military angle. We're heading to Canberra HQ in the morning. I have a friend..."

"Of course you do." Mom's military grapevine rivaled even the Commander's.

"I've told you that mahjongg is the great unifier," Mom replied.

I supposed I agreed. I'd met Holly at a game with Alice and Lena. "Thank you. This is above and beyond." What else could I say? It seemed so inadequate.

"Oh, honey. Everything will be okay. We will get to the bottom of this."

I believed her. I really did. I still bit my lip.

Sandy patted my arm. "We'll wait for your report from Canberra," she said, and disconnected the call. "Let's see what we get from the two families affected by the kidnapper's death."

I nodded, still overwhelmed.

Sandy's fingers raced across the computer keyboard. "Oh, man. Thornton's career spiraled downward after firing Lugger. His family lost their real estate holdings. His wife divorced him. No children. Just a niece and nephew. Wow! Thornton had been under consideration for a cabinet position. He was killed in a mugging two years later."

"That's convenient," I said dryly.

"I'll say. I just texted the chief. Colonel Morgan was the political liaison for the military to the cabinet. Lost a promising career as a lobbyist. His wife divorced him too. Geez, what ever happened to sticking with your man?"

"Don't look at me. I'll stand by Russ to the end." I would. No evidence would convince me he'd killed Lugger.

Satisfied, Sandy continued, "Morgan has two daughters. One graduated from the University of Sydney with a degree in art history. The younger daughter worked for De Beers at the time of the incident. No current employment history."

Holly with her big diamonds and eye for treasure came immediately to mind. Was she really interested in finding the treasure or just covering her tracks?

CHAPTER 16

We arrived at the villa before Aunt Char. Sandy set up both of her computers on the patio table facing the ocean. Not that I blamed her. Sunset painted the sky in every hue of red, orange, and blue while the dipping sun glowed over the azure ocean. I leaned against the rail and just stared, with Lizzie pressed to my side.

Aunt Char arrived as the fireball-sun dropped below the horizon. "It's lovely," she said quite calmly. Despite the heat and humidity, she appeared as neat as when we'd left her.

If not for Renny's cocky stance, I'd wonder if she'd left the air conditioning at all. "What did you find out?"

Aunt Char sat on the lounge chair. Renny jumped up beside her. "One moment, dear. I ordered..." Aunt Char's phone dinged. "Cocktails have arrived."

I stopped Sandy from dashing to the door. "I got it. I'm closest."

I opened the wooden door to find Tad, dressed in his usual shorts and a blue Cay polo shirt, carrying a bottle in each hand. Beside him stood a tall man whom I figured was a chef. The double-breasted black jacket with a Cay logo, as well as the platter of elegant canapés he held, confirmed it. The man sneezed, tipping his chef hat. Fortunately, the tray was covered with a clear lid.

Tad's usual smile seemed strained. "My apologies. I'll be back with a carrier. Chef is quite allergic to dogs."

I recognized those red, watery eyes. Russ practically lived with them in Barkview. I felt the man's pain, but who needed five-star service if it meant delaying Aunt Char's afternoon champagne or my shiraz?

I relieved Tad of the two bottles and stemware. Tad took the appetizers and released the chef. The man sneezed again and scurried away.

"Why would someone allergic to dogs work at Canine Cay?" I had to ask.

"Not many visiting dogs here. OZ's rules are strict. Lucas is very sensitive. He sneezed when he delivered something special to Villa one too," Tad said.

"Do they have dogs too?" I asked.

Tad brushed by me without answering. He set the appetizers on the bar while he prepared the drinks. Before serving us, Tad placed a silver water bowl and a plate at Renny's feet. "Chef prepared a chicken and blueberry treat for Miss Renny tonight."

The Queen Cavalier sniffed the bowl and rubbed her head against Tad's arm. I swear she swallowed the treats whole. Tad offered another to Lizzie, who also finished it in a single swallow.

I scribbled a Post-it reminder to get the recipe and stuffed it in my pocket. What I wouldn't pay for a good Renny bribe.

"Dinner'll be served at seven as requested, Mrs. Barklay. The Holmeses and Whiteses accepted your invitation for an after-dinner digestif. Mr. and Mrs. Blackman had not returned from their afternoon excursion when I left the kitchen. I'll find them."

Tad served Aunt Char a flute of champagne and Sandy and I the ruby shiraz. Cork-dork that I am, I spun the wine in my glass and inhaled. Bold blueberry mixed with blackberry filled my senses. I sipped the wine. I tasted the fresh fruit tempered with a spicy pepper.

Sandy's groan echoed my feelings. "Okay, I get your shiraz thing."

Ha. A convert. This was good stuff, made even better by the bold, salty Halloumi croquettes Tad offered us on crystal plates. The Gruyere he'd brought for Aunt Char hit the mark perfectly as well. We all moaned in pleasure as he retreated.

"Good heavens, Cat. We need to get Russ back immediately. I'll not have a stitch to wear otherwise." I ignored Aunt Char's mock complaint. I'd kill for her metabolism, which may not have been the right verb choice under the circumstances. Sandy's too. She might nod her agreement, but she never gained an ounce either. Talk about frustrating.

"Tell me what you found out," I said.

Aunt Char savored another sip of champagne and her cheese. "Your reclusive villa occupants do have a secret." The amusement twinkling in her sapphire-blue eyes didn't bode well for the kind of miracle Russ needed, though.

"What kind of secret?" I asked more sharply than intended. Disappointment did that to you.

"The occupant is a producer from California. He is here with his wife, preteen daughter, secretary, chef, and a tutor."

"I thought children weren't allowed here." Alice had said it. It must be true.

"Discouraged but not forbidden. As you would expect, the poor dear is quite bored. That's not the secret. The daughter smuggled in her Yorkie."

No wonder the chef had sneezed delivering there. "Aren't Yorkies nonallergic?"

Aunt Char nodded. "Some people are still sensitive, though."

"The teenager smuggled a real live dog?" Sandy asked.

"Yes. Ashley hid the dog in her Gucci backpack."

"How was that even possible?" Sure, a Yorkie is small, but Australian customs had been thorough on our arrival.

"I suppose when you arrive via private jet, customs is not as thorough." Aunt Char's sniff said more about the trouble she'd had with Renny than she'd admitted to. "Legally, the dog is in jeopardy. Australian law is quite strict regarding quarantine. The dog could easily be confiscated."

Sandy's hand over her mouth did not hide her gasp. "Why would she take a chance like that?"

"Selfishness, I imagine. She is only twelve, and I rather doubt she has experienced many boundaries." Aunt Char's opinions on parenting tended to be long-winded.

"Twelve is old enough to take responsibility," Sandy said.

"Her father's lawyers are looking for a solution," Aunt Char added.

"And you just happen to have one?" I recognized her problem-solved smile right away.

"Possibly. Bart Cathaway is a Yorkie short at next week's dog show," Aunt Char admitted.

The same Bart Cathaway who had cleared Renny's trip.

"Is the Yorkie even a show dog?" Despite my aunt's best intentions, this could be a disaster in the making.

"Fortunately, Bridget is a purebred." Aunt Char's frown indicated doubt. "Renny will do her best to get her ready. The dog has spark."

"But not the disposition," I finished for her. Aunt Char

should know; she'd successfully run the Barklay Kennel for a decade. "Will this subterfuge work?"

"No doubt, the dog is a bit of a mischief-maker. She knocked down the telescope. Has dug up some planters."

That explained the odd items Lugger had delivered there. "May I ask how you got in?"

Aunt Char stroked Renny's perfect white-spotted head. "She slipped through the fence."

The Queen Cavalier's preen concurred. The image didn't fit. My aunt's prissy dog squeeze through a fence for me? Never. It had to be about Russ.

"Naturally, I needed to retrieve her," Aunt Char said.

"Of course." Had to admire my aunt's tactics. She delivered every time.

"Ashley was quite excited that we visited. I looked through the telescope."

"Did she really see Lugger's murder? Or just make it up?" Cynicism from Sandy? She got along with everyone.

"Ashley saw someone wearing a Barkview hat, a blue shirt, and shorts. She never saw their face. She thought it was a man but swears they wore diamond earrings."

Sandy's gaze questioned mine. Could the diamond we'd found in Lugger's vehicle be a clue after all? "How did she know they wore earrings?"

"She saw sunlight sparkle at their ears," Aunt Char replied.

"Both ears?" I asked.

"Yes."

Assuming we'd found one of the earrings in Lugger's vehicle, that would mean that the killer had lost their earring after he'd been dropped on the beach.

"Still could be either male or female."

"True. The only person I recall wearing diamond earrings is

Holly. And there's no missing them," I replied. "Definitely not the one we found."

Sandy showed Aunt Char the stone inside the evidence bag.

"Ashley thought it was a man because he carried Lugger over his shoulders and staged him on the sand," Aunt Char said. "She specifically said 'staged.' Given her father's position, I imagine she knows a bit about that too."

That description set the scene well. "Lugger had to weigh two hundred twenty to two hundred thirty pounds. Only a strong man could've carried him."

"Or someone trained to carry deadweight in the fireman's carry," Sandy replied.

"A what?" I asked.

"You know. It's when an injured person is laid across both shoulders. It's a standard military carry when transporting injured soldiers. You've seen pictures..." She tapped on her computer and then turned the screen for both Aunt Char and me to see.

"You know how to do that?" I asked.

"Yes. I dated a lifeguard."

Of course she had. I had the perfect visual of Lugger now. "Even using the carry, there's no way I'm getting a guy outweighing me by eighty pounds on my shoulders. Never mind stage him."

Sandy reluctantly agreed.

Lizzie nudged my thigh. "Good point. Where were you? If you'd been there, you would've fought back."

No missing Aunt Char and Sandy's gapes. Yeah, I was talking to a dog. I would swear Lizzie was smarter than me anyway. At least sometimes.

"Ashley said Lizzie arrived about fifteen minutes after the

man left Lugger. The dog came running from the main building."

"She came from Lugger's place." The timing fit Zed's story perfectly. "How did the guy leave?"

"Ashley said he arrived in an aluminum boat with a platypus on the bow," Aunt Char said.

My heart thumped. "A platypus? Is she sure?"

Sandy showed us a picture of the animal.

"That is what Ashley described. She also told me that the males are venomous. Which I thought quite apropos," Aunt Char said.

"I know where to find the boat." Both women and two dogs stared at me. "Every room is assigned an EV and a boat. Each one has a painted animal on the bow. I don't know who was assigned the platypus, but I know who to ask."

"I saw the boats on the beach when we arrived," Sandy added. "The area didn't appear secured. Any cameras, by chance?"

I shook my head. "You're kidding, right? This is an island known for privacy and discretion." Not unlike Barkview.

"Someone must've seen something," Sandy insisted.

"At dawn, when you're on vacation?" Only Russ got up with the sun.

"What about the fishermen? They tend to leave early." Sandy wasn't giving up. I liked that about her.

"Holly's husband booked the morning trip. He canceled at the last minute," I replied.

"The Holly who doesn't exist?" Sandy twisted her long blonde hair into a ponytail. "Why didn't Ashley call the police right away?"

Indignation surrounded Aunt Char's exhale. "She thought the man lying on the beach had just passed out. The poor dear has far too much experience with that."

No doubt a Barkview intervention loomed. Sandy saw it too. There was no point fighting Aunt Char on a mission.

"So, we're looking for a man with a small head who wears a diamond earring," Sandy concluded.

"Who also managed to somehow lock up Lizzie in Lugger's apartment." I scratched the Aussie's suddenly alert head. If only she could talk.

"Lizzie must know him," Sandy said.

Aussie fur flew when Lizzie left my side to rub against Sandy. I wasn't sure why I felt abandoned. What did I care if the dog shed on someone else for a change?

Aunt Char's phone pinged. "Ah, Gregory has arrived with the FBI investigators." Years of friendship afforded Aunt Char the privilege of calling Uncle G by his given name. Not that I'd ever dared. Uncle G worked just fine.

Good news or bad, I wasn't sure. Too much evidence still incriminated Russ.

"Do you mind moving in here with Sandy and me?" Aunt Char asked. "It is best that Gregory has his own space."

"Of course. I'll just pick up a few things." I'd planned to crash here anyway. Without Russ, the beachfront room depressed me.

"Excellent." Aunt Char turned serious. "No talking to the FBI without Russ's lawyer present. Gregory will manage that investigation."

No argument from me, though the FBI might have something to say about that. Uncle G would filter the information that needed to be sent their direction.

Aunt Char pointed to Sandy. "You will be at Cat's side at all times. Never, ever leave her alone."

A Sandy guard? Both Lizzie and I took instant offense. Lizzie barked her objection. Renny cut her off with a firm bark of her own that sent Lizzie into a huff. This alpha-dog thing intrigued me. How could a Cavalier a quarter of the Aussie's size rule the room?

The same way Aunt Char did, I realized. My aunt had my best interests in mind. I respected that. Sandy looked even less excited about the task than me. Not that I blamed her. Restrictions rarely held me in check.

"Why?" I asked.

"Gregory and I suspect there is more to this rush to judgment by the local authorities."

Her words shook me to the core. "You think there is another agenda?"

Aunt Char sipped her champagne. "I see no reason to take a chance."

She knew something. Despite my prodding, she'd say no more. I trusted her judgment more than my own right now.

We talked about my mother's findings before heading to dinner at the Look Out. While Aunt Char and Sandy changed for dinner, Lizzie and I paced on the veranda, staring down at the dark beach below. In the morning, we would have a real chance to follow the murderer's escape route.

CHAPTER 17

Uncle G arrived at the villa driving a four-seater EV. Standing well over six feet tall and blessed with linebacker shoulders, he intimidated in his neatly-pressed shorts and Barkview Police polo, despite his full head of silver hair and Santa Claus beard.

His bear hug scared me as much as it comforted. "Russ sends his love. He instructed me to remind you to trust your instincts."

I bit my lip, suddenly overwhelmed. If only I trusted them myself. The stakes were so much higher than puzzling together an intriguing adventure.

Aunt Char's hand on my shoulder touched my soul. "Breathe, my dear. All of us as one..."

Lizzie's bark broke the tension. "And you too, Lizzie. We will all solve this together." Aunt Char motioned Sandy to join the group hug.

We being the operative word.

Uncle G's gruff voice reinforced it. "Don't overthink. Just let your intuition lead you."

If only it was that easy. Coolness in a crisis wasn't in my DNA. "Did you find out anything odd?" I finally asked.

Uncle G nodded. "Lugger's place in Cairns was tossed three weeks ago. He reported nothing missing, but whoever did it was looking for something specific."

"How do you know?" I asked.

"The crime scene photos showed cereal boxes and ice trays dumped. Walls cut open. Floorboards lifted. Lamps shattered," Uncle G explained.

"Did anyone see anything?" Sandy asked.

Uncle G shook his head. "No cameras. No police investigation either. I canvassed traffic cams. Tracked a white Range Rover reported stolen in the area. Lost it when it left the city center. Never got a good angle. Both occupants wore bush hats. One passenger appeared to be wearing earrings."

"Diamond earrings?" I asked.

"The reflection indicated as much. Why?"

"The witness who identified Russ also saw someone wearing diamond earrings," Aunt Char said.

Now the tough question—the one Uncle G didn't want to answer. "Why are the police still holding Russ? I know he tested negative for GSR."

Uncle G's exhale didn't ruffle my calm. "The constabulary discovered payments from the US to Lugger spanning the past five years."

"Blackmail." My heart sank. "Since the Torres Strait Islander's death."

"That's the theory. They haven't linked the payments to Russ yet."

"And that's why Cat hasn't been arrested too," Aunt Char added.

"Russ denies it. The FBI is tracing the wire transfers. The best computer minds are working on this."

I really wanted to believe that. "Do you think this was an inside job?" Russ would not be happy if someone in his office was involved.

"Possibly. The long game interests me here. Someone has been setting Lugger and Russ up for some time."

"What kind of person waits five years to exact revenge?" I asked.

"The really mad kind," Sandy replied. "And dangerous."

True. "How much money are we talking about?"

"Enough that Lugger should've been living either a more extravagant lifestyle or have a healthy savings account, which he does not."

Now that I believed. I also had a pretty good idea who'd been assigned the platypus boat. Lugger's murder had definitely been personal. "Sandy, send a note to Jennifer. We need everything she can dig up on Randall Thornton, his ex-wife and his niece and nephew, and on Colonel Morgan and his daughters."

Sandy beelined to her laptop. "It's 1 a.m. in Barkview." She waited for my nod.

I hated to wake anyone up, but revenge was a dangerous motive.

Uncle G typed on his phone as well. "The FBI is good for something." Spoken like a true loner cop.

"We need to check on the platypus boat," I said.

I let Aunt Char explain while the four of us and two dogs squeezed into the EV. Renny lounged comfortably on Aunt Char's lap, while Lizzie sprawled over me. Her back paws on the seat and front on my chest, I blew fur out of my mouth, waiting for a break in Sandy's typing.

We arrived at the Look Out in time to observe at least three shadows in a heated discussion on the beach beside the skiffs. My heart skipped a beat. Were we too late? Had the FBI's arrival spooked them? No planes had left the island, but anyone could escape by boat.

Lizzie jumped off my lap before Uncle G stopped. I sprinted after her, forcing Sandy to abandon her search-in-progress and give chase.

No niceties, I stuck my head into the group consisting of Emma, Fin, and Coop. "Can you find them?" I panted. I could barely catch my breath. Playing pickleball regularly clearly didn't qualify me as being in good shape.

"Yeah. We have their GPS coordinates." Fin's confidence worked for me.

"Real time?" Sandy asked.

Fin nodded. "For safety. We don't advertise it, but guests do lose their way and sea conditions can be unpredictable. On occasion we need to locate them."

No judgment on my part. "Where is the boat now?"

Fin referred to the device he held. "Offshore near the Cod Hole. They must be out of fuel and caught in the current. I'll go after them in the sportfisher."

Uncle G arrived, not the least bit winded, his situation assessment right on. "The FBI can get a chopper up from Cairns."

"*Fin's Caster* will arrive faster. Excuse me."

A man and a woman dressed entirely in black sprinted across the sand. "We'd like a lift, mate," the gentleman said.

Fin gestured for them to follow him down the dock. Lizzie crouched, ready to join them too. I froze, not exactly sure what to do. Emma stepped up and called the dog back. Lizzie whined and turned those big, blue, beseeching eyes on me. Ugh! Talk about manipulation. I crossed my arms. I couldn't give in.

"Was it the platypus?" Sandy's question cleared the air.

Emma nodded. "Yeah. How'd you know?"

"Holly and her husband aren't who they claim to be." Granted, we didn't know exactly who they were, but...

Emma chuckled, less concerned. "Many people come here for anonymity."

"And murder." Sandy covered her mouth too late.

"Crickey!" Emma's clipboard hit the sand.

A realization hit me before I could comfort her. "The Cod Hole is near the edge of Australia's international waters. What happens if they pass it?"

"Maritime law doesn't allow us to arrest them if they board another country's vessel," Uncle G said. "The boat's registry then dictates the rules."

"No worries. They're short on petrol," Emma insisted.

"Check your fuel reserve." Uncle G's growl penetrated Emma's denial.

She did. Her gasp said it all. Holly was on the run. Uncle G grumbled as he called in reinforcements. He hung up a moment later. "We'll need to see their room."

Emma acquiesced in less than a second. No reason to allow it without a warrant—if that's the way it worked in Australia —but refusing Uncle G anything took real courage, the kind a rattled Emma didn't seem to have without Fin at her side.

She motioned us to follow her. Located two doors from the room I'd shared with Russ, Holly's suite was also decorated with a relaxed ocean-air feel. Although lush tropical foliage that included flowering pink ginger plants separated the suites, backlighting offered full visibility. Note to self: always close the shutters and put away your dirty laundry.

This suite looked as if the occupants had gone out in a rush but intended to return. Shorts dangled off chair backs, while kicked-off flip-flops lay where they'd landed. A bikini even dried on the bathroom doorknob. Resort clothing still hung in the closet and filled the drawers.

Had I been wrong? This didn't look like a couple bent on escape.

Uncle G handed us all blue gloves. "Touch nothing."

I didn't ask why we needed the gloves. It was easier just to go along.

"No laptop or cameras," Sandy announced.

"Cosmetics and sunscreen are accounted for." I half expected Aunt Char to salute.

"Safe empty," Uncle G said. "Except for this." He handed me a silver jeweler's loupe, tweezers, and a four-inch-long black box with a pen-like probe and light gauges.

"What is that?" Sandy peered at the odd box.

"A diamond meter. This uses a thermal conductor to determine if a stone is a natural diamond or not." I'd used it in a diamond-grading class at the Gemological Institute of America. Anyone working at De Beer's would be intimately familiar with it.

Emma collapsed into a chair. "They murdered Lugger for the Dakota Diamonds?"

I wanted to believe it, but something felt wrong about this scene. I held the loupe to the light. The inscription caught my eye. "To HM with love, The Colonel." My heart thumped. HM could stand for Holland Morgan, the court-martialed Colonel Morgan's daughter. No way this was a coincidence.

"When did the Blackmans book their room?"

"They booked on Monday," Emma stuttered. "And arrived on the flight you missed from Cairns."

It all started to make sense. We'd had delays in customs in Sydney, which had caused us to miss the connecting flight. Had that been orchestrated?

"How could they have known we were coming here? I didn't even know." Both Aunt Char and Sandy refused to meet my eyes. "Okay. When did you two know?"

"Russ has been planning this since your engagement," Aunt Char admitted. "It was quite romantic."

I'd feel happy later when it all made sense. "But we got married on twenty-four hours' notice."

Again, both women smiled. "He couldn't have pulled it off without preplanning."

Which meant... "Who else knew?"

Sandy's blush confirmed that everyone except me had known.

Great. Too many possibilities. The timing still didn't make total sense, but maybe... The big picture came back to me with a vengeance. Someone had been setting up Lugger's death for a long time. "They had no reason to kill Lugger."

"Everyone had some reason to kill Lugger," Emma mumbled.

I'd heard that before. All eyes turned to Emma until Uncle G's phone rang. "Maritime Border Command just picked up the platypus. They are thirty minutes out."

Emma sank into a plush and clothing-free side chair. "They're safe."

Relief should've washed over me too. Catching Lugger's killer would vindicate Russ, yet his freedom didn't feel guaranteed.

Uncle G's question seemed to concur. "Why did everyone have some reason to kill Lugger?"

Emma's classic deer-in-the-headlights look showed real fear. "I misspoke."

"You did not." I had to admire his relentlessness when provoked. "Why did you want to kill Lugger?"

"I-I..." She buried her face in her hands. "He encouraged Meryl to return to university."

Aunt Char waved us away. No problem. Psychoanalysis

was her department. "What does Meryl want?" she asked in her usual lulling, nonthreatening, yet prying manner.

"Someone else can advocate for the whales. She's the soul of the Pearl Farm. She's destined to be here," Emma said. "The dingo spirit speaks through her. The Cay is her home."

Destined or coerced? I'd felt the pull of the spirit too, but not that kind of pressure. Ever attuned to me, Lizzie snuck her head reassuringly beneath my hand.

"Who else would want to kill Lugger?" Aunt Char asked.

"Lugger delivered Coop's reserve shiraz to all the area winery competitions. Offers have been drawing him to leave for months."

"You're afraid he will accept one," Aunt Char said gently.

Emma nodded. "He belongs here at the Cay, building this land for his children like our granddad and father did."

"Keeping your family together is important to you, Emma, isn't it?" Aunt Char asked.

"Yeah. We have a responsibility to our children to continue..." Tears choked her words.

No need to point out that there was no next generation yet. Aunt Char's lulling voice continued. "Lugger believed in doing what you love. Do you love managing the Cay?"

"Indeed. I..." The words sounded untrue even to my untrained ears. Tears rolled down Emma's cheek.

"What do you dream of?" my aunt asked.

The lack of an answer didn't deter my aunt. "Interior design, perhaps? You have a beautiful eye." My aunt gestured all around us.

The spell broke. "How did you...?"

"There is much to see if you look at what is right in front of you."

Aunt Char's wisdom resonated. She did see things others

missed. Was that what Lugger meant when he'd penned the note?

Beneath the surface you will find deeper meaning.

Were his words intended for all of us to ponder? This lack of answers bugged me like an itch I couldn't quite scratch. Every minute I reached for relief, Russ remained in prison.

If Emma had killed Lugger, she would have needed help. Which really got us nowhere. With any luck, Holly would fit the bill.

CHAPTER 18

The sportfisher towed the platypus to the dock, followed by what could only be called a BGB. That's a big gray boat, the likes of which filled San Diego Harbor and Pearl Harbor under US Navy jurisdiction. And total overkill to return two runaways in an aluminum skiff.

"Impressive, huh?" Uncle G whispered. "Australians consider border security a priority. That's an Armidale-class cruiser."

Like I said, suited for the US Navy. The boat appeared to be well over one hundred and fifty feet in length and maybe thirty feet wide. The narrow-bowed boat dropped anchor and floated just outside the cove in ominous glory. Talk about an intimidating deterrent.

Uncle G took the bow line and cleated *Fin's Caster*'s lines with practiced precision. "You're a boater?" I cleated the stern line.

"Offshore ocean sailor in my day. I sailed in the TransPac race from San Pedro, California, to Hawaii." His grin told of good times.

"Oh, I see. In the square sail days." Had to tease him. The man's accomplishments were many and varied.

"Argh. A pirate's life for me."

"Eh, matie," said Fin as he climbed onto the dock.

"What happened?" Uncle G asked.

Fin gestured toward the border security boat. "Big boat won." He checked our lines and walked toward the Cay.

My smile froze in place when the government's dual-outboard dinghy arrived for tie-up a few minutes later. If the boat's arrival didn't make a big enough scene, Lizzie leaping like a flyfish from the dock onto the boat and barking sure did. Every eye from the Look Out bored into my back.

Holly's command shut the dog down with Renny's Queen Cavalier ease. I really needed to master that tone. When she marched off the dinghy, her flashing blue eyes sliced right through me as if this was all my fault.

Undaunted, I glared right back. No handcuffs? My confidence balked.

The FBI agents exited. "If there is anything we can assist with, Inspector Morgan, don't hesitate to ask."

"Inspector?" The word about stuck in my throat.

"Ruh roh." Sandy's whisper hit me hard.

No kidding. What had I done?

"You singlehandedly undermined an eighteen-month high-level smuggling investigation." Holly's pointed finger might as well have been a blade.

"Smugglers operating at the Cay?" Impossible. Not on this idyllic tropical island.

Holly handed Uncle G an official-looking badge. "Make your confirmation calls. Your FBI brethren were satisfied." She gestured for Sandy, Aunt Char, and me to follow her. Confused, we did, while Uncle G talked on his phone in hushed tones.

We did our best to ignore the clothing clutter as Uncle G

confirmed Holly's identity. "You're cleared to share your case details."

"Naturally. You do have friends in high places." Holly poured two drams of whiskey. She downed the first herself and handed the other to the tall, dark-haired man who materialized beside her. "This is my partner, Josh. He'll be happy to get back to his family."

No missing the man's grimace. Going home without results chafed. I got it.

Holly poured another shot. "I'm not at all certain if you and your husband have bad honeymoon karma or your presence is mere interference."

"You walked into an international diamond-smuggling operation," Uncle G said.

It took a second to process that tidbit.

"I'm the ranking inspector investigating stolen diamonds in the Australian Federal Police," Holly admitted.

"You're Colonel Morgan's daughter." My tone just dared her to deny it.

"Quite right. Deduced that, did you? My father's choices did inspire my career."

"You expect me to believe your involvement in this case is a coincidence." I looked to Uncle G for support. He believed less in chance than I did. Too bad his shrug didn't help at all.

"It's the truth. Life's path does on occasion bring you full circle."

That bit of reason made too much sense. I still wasn't entirely convinced. Not by a long shot. "Go on."

"We've been tracking Lugger T for eighteen months. He's what you Americans would call a mule. He picked up loose diamonds..."

"What diamonds?" Now I was confused. The Dakota Diamonds reportedly had been here for eighty years.

"Argyle diamonds. Stolen from the mine in 2019. We started seeing them in Europe six months ago. Our sources tell us the latest shipment appears to be from the newer Merlin Mine. The diamonds are round brilliants, D color, VVS1 quality or better. They range in size from half to one carat."

"Easily sold." Even I knew the average stone fit those criteria.

"Yeah. The diamonds were retrieved from various unlikely suppliers. Lugger gathered the stones and delivered them to the Cay. The trail goes cold here. Day before yesterday, we marked the last shipment."

"Marked it how?" Sandy asked.

"A nanoparticulate spray," Josh explained.

My turn to frown.

"It's a spray that gives off a distinct spectral signature and can be tracked with a simple infrared scanner or drone," Holly explained.

'We found a diamond in Lugger's EV." I motioned Sandy to show Holly the evidence-bagged diamond.

Josh louped the stone and used the diamond meter. With a nod, he confirmed the diamond's origin.

Holly chewed her lip. "Sloppy."

"A setup?" I suggested.

"The Cay's the perfect smugglers haven. They have frequent visitors. No law to speak of," Holly agreed.

No kidding. Rog hardly resembled diligence, waiting out his time for retirement.

"Today we saw two boats—apparently dive boats—sitting off the Cod Hole. We were watching to see if the Cod Hole is a drop."

"You suspect Fin's involvement?" I asked.

"It's quite possible that the stones are stashed underwater and retrieved by divers or a mini-sub. That's what you interrupted. Fin disappeared during the Cod Hole dive yesterday. We've had eyes on the site since. We didn't find diamonds, but there was a white line floating on the outer edge of the reef. May be a signal."

Which I had interrupted. Great. Loyal Fin a smuggler? Wouldn't be the first time I'd misjudged someone, but...

"We've investigated the winery. Their two mainland distributors appear clean. Majority of the products are consumed on the Cay. Nothing is exported," Holly said.

"Nothing unusual in the distribution chain either," Josh added.

Disappointing.

"We also looked into the Pearl Farm. Although the Cay Pearls are shipped internationally, the farm itself works with a single long-term distributor in Brisbane. The pearls are sent to the factory, which sets them and returns a small percentage here for local sale. The rest are sold through high-end jewelry stores worldwide."

"We've run numerous stings," Josh said. "We've found nothing. No one suspicious either."

Talk about frustrating. How could diamonds just vanish on a small island? I glanced at Sandy. I could see her mind wrestling with the same question.

Suddenly, Sandy stood. "You said the signature vanished. Would liquid interfere with the signal? Like hiding them in wine barrels?"

All eyes turned on her. "Yeah. We've spot-checked all transported wine bottles."

"Even the bottles sent to competitions?" I asked. The quantity would be small. Easy to miss.

Holly and Josh's glance said I'd hit on something.

"The timing fits." I got Sandy's point right away. "The reserve shiraz is barreled for three years." Simple math told the rest of the tale. That would explain why diamonds stolen over four years ago started showing up six months ago.

Holly got it. So did Josh. He exited quickly, calling for backup as he left.

With any luck, they'd find something. The sawdust I'd brushed off my knees after leaving the winery came immediately to mind. Oak barrels gave off sawdust. I remembered that tidbit from a Central Valley winery tour. Since I hadn't visited the barrel storage area when I'd been there, the only place I could've knelt in the sawdust was while attempting to get through Lizzie's doggie door at Lugger's place. Was it a clue or a coincidence?

Hope surged through me. Holly crushed it in a heartbeat. "The winery's a long shot. We've also looked at frequent guests."

"The Whites and Holmeses?" Could smug Alice be a diamond diva? Lena had secrets and a young family.

"Among others. Nothing unusual there either."

"Lugger was your only link?" I asked. Something just felt wrong.

"We got him when we flipped a local dealer," Holly admitted.

"Lugger did run a pickup and delivery service. Maybe he didn't know," I reminded her out of loyalty to the man who'd helped my husband.

"Then why murder him? Current theory's that he wanted out. Lugger started cleaning up his act in preparation for your husband's imminent arrival," Holly said.

It still didn't feel right.

"Who broke into Lugger's place?" Uncle G asked.

"A local thief. We've been watching him. Hasn't led us anywhere yet. Lugger's neighbor called the constables. Lugger wasn't surprised."

"You're suggesting that he knew the who and why?" I asked of no one in particular. All clues still led us right back to the Cay. Someone on the island had to be the mastermind. One of the sibling owners? Sweet Emma? Make-the-best-of-it Coop or resigned Meryl? Were they really that unhappy?

"Tad seems to have access to everything." He showed up everywhere, ready to help and always discreet.

Holly shrugged. "We've looked into Zed and Lily too. Nothing to report."

"Why don't you think that the Torres Strait incident is involved?" I asked.

Holly rolled her eyes. "Not everything's a conspiracy."

Not in my experience. Revenge was a great motivator.

"And if the Dakota Diamonds ever existed, they are long gone." Spoken like a real-life investigator.

"We're missing something," Sandy remarked.

As usual, we were on the same page. "The frame on Russ is too personal. There is more than smuggling diamonds going on." My intuition agreed with a vengeance.

"Your husband was an easy distraction. With the FBI, Federal Police, and Cairns Constabulary investigating, I suspect he will be cleared shortly."

I wanted to believe her. "How shortly?" Forget my hesitation. I knew I liked her.

"When the time's right."

I liked her confidence. "What does that mean, exactly?"

"For the purposes of the investigation, I'd rather he stay where he is. Let the smuggler hold onto a false sense of security. He'll make a mistake."

"He hasn't since you started the investigation." At this rate, Russ could be locked up in an Australian prison for life! Not that it mattered. My husband would never jeopardize an ongoing investigation anyway.

Diminished concern about the ultimate outcome did wonders for my Zen, though.

Aunt Char stood. "A few guests will be joining us for after-dinner drinks at the villa. Join us. Perhaps there will be clarity."

I doubted that. The more I learned, the more confusing this case became.

CHAPTER 19

Lizzie and I tiptoed out of the villa a little before dawn. No sense waking Aunt Char and Sandy. Though I doubted they'd hear me over the snoring coming through both of their doors. Acclimating to Australian time was no easy task. Why else would don't-talk-to-me-before-nine me already be on my feet after a night when I tossed and turned, my mind filled with too many possibilities?

I brushed aside Aunt Char's request that I not go out alone. She'd said that before I'd outed Holly, and I really didn't want to bother Sandy. Without her hyperactive Jack Russell Terrier interfering, she could relax. Besides, Lizzie was with me.

Me, the coffeeholic, didn't even stop to brew a joe. Had to be a testament to my mixed-up state of mind. I just knew I had to get out.

In the driveway, I eyed my EV, parked beside Aunt Char's. That obnoxious back-up screech would wake up the entire area. There had to be another way to move it. How else had Lugger left his place without waking Zed the morning he'd been murdered? I pressed the electric start button and tried pushing. It didn't even budge. The bent ginger flower paid the price for my driving-in-a-tight-circle idea. I finally admitted defeat and drove Aunt Char's four-seater. Uncle G, truck owner that he was, had backed into his parking spot, making my getaway complete.

That can't-be-missed back-up sound was unmistakable. Yet Zed claimed to have not heard Lugger's the morning he'd died.

Impossible. Why had he lied? And sawdust had been found near Lugger's body and in front of Lugger's door. The evidence definitely pointed to his involvement. But why? What possible motive could Zed have for killing Lugger?

Lizzie rode beside me, her tongue catching the breeze as I sped into the predawn light toward the airport. I arrived just as morning's first rays teased the horizon, promising another magical tropical day. Bouncing headlights like beady eyes came right at me from the Pearl Farm trail. Heart pounding, I turned off the road and felt inside the center console until I located the binoculars.

The vehicle skidded to a stop in front of the A frame. Zed, dressed in last night's stained and rumpled clothing, stumbled out of the vehicle, slid open the door, and drove in. No reason to close the door. He'd completed the walk of shame.

I bit back a smile. Zed and Lily or Meryl? Odd that I'd heard no gossip to confirm or deny it. A nightly rendezvous would explain why he hadn't heard Lugger's vehicle. He hadn't been in the building.

Another puzzle piece fell neatly into place. Not that the info would help to release Russ. Lizzie knew it too. Front paws on the dash, she looked ready for action as we bumped down the trail toward the Pearl Farm. Maybe there was something to Russ's early-bird thing. If he was here, I'd even give it a try.

I pinkie-wiped a tear. It would all work out. I had faith. It had to.

I turned off the path at the Pearl Farm lookout. Although the FBI had confiscated Lugger's EV for further analysis, the empty space still affected me as I drove by.

Lizzie exited when I stopped, patiently waiting for me at the trail while I tied my hair back with my tiger-print scarf and grabbed the binoculars. Why not? Who knew what dawn bird-watching opportunities would present themselves? Yikes. Did that make me an official birder? Not that anyone in Barkview would ever believe it. I'm not sure I did.

Lizzie hugged my leg as we walked in step toward the colorful sunrise. The sound of seabirds and heat on my face warmed my bones. I didn't miss California's chilly morning clouds one bit.

I'd spotted a pair of crested terns when Lizzie nudged my hand and barked. At least I think it was Lizzie's bark that drew my eye to the cove. The pearl boat was already out. Meryl had said they'd start harvesting and seeding the oysters early. She hadn't been kidding.

I recognized Lily from yesterday, dressed in another shorty wetsuit with her braid reaching halfway down her back. The second person... I adjusted the binoculars. Was that Meryl bent over the tub? She'd seemed taller yesterday.

Lizzie barked again and bolted down a half-hidden trail. "Lizzie. Come!" I yelled.

A lot of good it did. The Aussie never looked back. I really hated it when a dog disobeyed.

Me, chase another dog into who knew what mess? Not this time. I'd paid the bad-behavior price chasing both a Golden Doodle and a Corgi into an unknown situation. A third time would be insanity.

I glanced down at the idyllic bay. Was I just being paranoid? How much danger could a single workboat represent anyway?

Lizzie's I'm-waiting bark overrode my doubts. As if I ever really had a choice.

I dialed Sandy as I ran. Of course, the call went to voice-mail, saying a lot about just how exhausted she was. I left a quick message detailing my location and plan before disconnecting the call. She'd join us if she wanted to re-nucleate the oysters.

Blazing my own trail after the Aussie took my full concentration. No wonder Sandy and I had missed this path. Only a machete would've saved me from the many scratches I suffered as I traversed the twisty-turny, overgrown, exposed roots and loose rock path that led to the Pearl Farm. I arrived to find Lizzie stutter-stepping on the dock and barking like a lunatic. Something wasn't right. I could feel it.

Lily's emphatic wave was no invitation. The dog tossed me a look and long-jumped into the water. Her belly flop doused me. Come on!

"Lizzie. No. Come." My I'm-the-alpha tone failed. The dog ignored me. Fear drove me to act. If the Aussie messed up the sensitive nucleation process...

I leaped into the scuba-ready zodiac tied to the dock and pulled the engine starter. Not even a choke. I tried again. Nothing. The third time did it. The engine hummed at the cost of my gel manicure. The ripped nail tore completely off as I unslipped the lines, pointing the boat at the dog paddling toward the pearl boat.

The Aussie beat me by a hair. I rounded the pearl boat's stern as Lizzie fell backward off the ladder and sank underwater. Was that red cloud blood in the water, or just her collar's reflection? No reason to panic. Except the dog wasn't surfacing!

My teenage lifeguard training took over. I kicked off my pickleball shoes, grabbed the diving mask with attached snorkel stacked with the scuba gear, and dove in. I found Lizzie right away, suspended in the water. Not moving at all.

My adrenalin pumping on high, I grabbed the Aussie and pulled her to the surface. I rolled the dog onto her back and towed her to the pearl boat's stern platform. Lizzie still hadn't moved. She wasn't breathing!

I automatically covered the dog's nose with my mouth and exhaled. Once. Twice. Three times.

Lizzie coughed. So did I, and spat out fur too. Ick. Ick! What was I thinking? I wiped my lips, tasting salt and something metallic. Geez. The dog really had been hurt.

I untied my scarf and pressed it to a cut at the back of her neck. "Hey. Some help here," I screamed. "Lizzie's been hurt." Still holding onto the dog, I pulled myself up onto the first ladder rung.

Hands on her hips, Lily stood there. "You bloody Yank."

What the...? No time to ask. The pointed end of a speargun aimed at me said it all. Up close, I recognized Lily's companion as the dog-allergic chef. Although he wore no earrings, piercing holes marked his earlobe. In fact, the resemblance between him and Lily was uncanny. Twins. The disgraced Thursday Island mayor's elusive niece and nephew?

It all made perfect sense now. No wonder Holly hadn't found the stolen Argyle Mine's diamonds. They'd been hidden in plain sight all along, seeded into the Cay's internationally acclaimed pearls and openly shipped worldwide. Brilliant plan, actually. Best money-laundering operation ever. How had Lily ever thought of it? It hit me then. Great ideas rarely came around once. I knew exactly where the Dakota Diamonds were.

Not that it mattered. One look at the receiving end of that

barbed spear, and I empathized with an about-to-be-dinner fish. I fell back into the water. What only could be described as net pods weighted with oysters attached to moored ropes swayed in the water like giant California kelp around me. I thought about hiding among the many lines until a spear shot by me, missing by a less-than-comfortable margin.

Who knew I'd ever curse excellent visibility? In this case, it made me an easy target. I looked wildly around. The zodiac offered some cover.

I grabbed a panting Lizzie and dove. The dog wasn't having any of it. She jerked out of my grasp and paddled in the opposite direction, barking with Doberman ferocity. I had no choice. I'd have to get to the inflatable boat and come back for her.

The hiss of rapidly escaping air greeted my arrival. One of those scary spears stuck out of the bow, ending my half-formed escape plan. This boat wasn't going anywhere. I treaded water, watching the rubber pontoon boat list.

Wait a minute. I hid as best I could behind the deflating pontoon and reached into the cockpit. I pulled out Meryl's just-in-case scuba equipment and fins. It took less than a minute to turn on the air, slip my arms into the buoyancy compensator, and pull on the fins. I dove just in time. A spear whizzed by my shoulder as I surfaced under the sinking boat. My air gauge showed 1,500 psi. I was safe, for now.

Lizzie wasn't. Her water-logged yelp sounded desperate. I dove deep and swam underwater, through the suspended pouches of oysters swaying beneath the boat, until I saw the Aussie flailing in the water.

I swam beneath the dog, grabbed her by the collar, and pulled her underwater. The next spear missed by a smaller margin. Their rapidly-improving aim wasn't comforting me any.

I resurfaced in the air pocket under the drooping zodiac

and tied a standard life vest around the dog. It wasn't a perfect fit, but Lizzie floated. She licked my face, exhausted. We were both okay...but for how long, who knew? I needed a long-term solution.

Disabling the pearl boat and forcing Lily and her companion to swim to shore made the most sense. If I dove deep and came up under the boat, I could cut off the engine's fuel supply. How hard could it be? Hollywood did it all the time.

I ordered Lizzie to stay and dove deep. Before I completely disconnected the fuel line, another arrow zoomed by me, this time snagging my buoyance compensator's armhole and propelling my shoulder backward. Pain sliced through my shoulder moments before I saw the blood—my blood. I'd been hit!

I screamed like an overwhelmed rookie diver. A mouthful of saltwater snapped me out of it. Panic killed more divers than the water. Of course, most divers didn't have a deadly spear gunning for them. Staying put wasn't an option, though. The next spear could get me. I tried to dive deeper, but the oyster pod ropes held me in place. My shoulder was pinned—the spear had grazed my arm and passed through the BCD, piercing its air bladder and embedding in the rope. That I'd get no buoyancy from that device didn't scare me too much. I could swim to the surface. The waterline wasn't far; I could see it.

I tried to untangle the mess, but the spear tip had lodged in the rope. Escape meant leaving the BCD and air tank behind.

It took a second, but I calmed my racing heart and checked my gauges. Depth: nineteen meters. I'd blown half my air supply and lost a fin. I was alive, but for how long? Lily's aim improved with every shot.

I waited a few seconds for them to take another shot. Nothing. Could they be out of spears? Hope washed over me until I looked around.

What was that in the distance? I'd only glimpsed a blur. Shaped like a shovel... OMG! I brushed small droplets of blood off my shoulder. Meryl had said these were shark-infested waters!

No wonder Lily and her companion hadn't shot me. The shark would take care of it for them!

That shadowy blur flashed in and out of my vision again, closer than the last time.

No! I had a deal with sharks. I didn't eat them if they didn't eat me. I'd lived up to my end. Their turn to do their part!

I'd lost my mind for sure. Every shark documentary I'd ever seen played back in my mind. I knew the fish's MO. It circled, methodically moving in until I weakened. The moment I swam for the surface, the shark would strike from below.

My heart pounded in my ears. I looked around. The creepy absence of other fish confirmed my hypothesis. They'd sensed what was coming and taken cover. The swaying ropes wouldn't protect me at all. Neither would the sandy bottom, which had few rocks and no hiding places. The smell of blood would lead the shark right to me anyway.

I wasn't getting out of this one, I realized with an oddly calm finality. It's true what they say about your life flashing before your eyes—the good, the bad, and all the stuff you wished you'd done. I refused to cry. I'd made my choices. At least I'd married Russ and made up with my mother. I wished we'd all had more time together.

A shadow blocked the light above for a brief second. I looked toward the surface and prayed for Russ. He'd promised just a few days ago to always meet me halfway. No. He was in prison because I'd failed him.

Momentary hope shattered. Nothing was up there. To

make matters worse, insistent, give-you-a-headache barking pounded through my head. Lizzie? Had that crazy dog paddled from safety out into the open again in a futile attempt to protect me? I couldn't let her do it. I was almost out of air anyway. It was time...

My hand shook as I unhooked the BC, took one last deep breath, and slowly exhaled as I kicked for the surface. I closed my eyes. No need to see the attack coming. It would all be over quickly. I wouldn't feel a thing.

In the end, I saw nothing. The feverish barking got louder and louder, practically pulling me to the surface until I exhaled the last of my air. My lungs felt ready to explode. Saltwater trickled into my mouth. OMG! I was going to drown.

Russ, I love you.

Suddenly, his arms were around me. I had to be dead but wasn't. My husband pulled me out of the water and saved my life. Confirming, without a doubt, that marrying him had been the best decision I'd ever made.

CHAPTER 20

I had the FBI computer guys to thank for proving Russ hadn't blackmailed Lugger, and Holly for arranging his dawn helicopter ride to the Cay. Lizzie's heroic swim had marked my location, and I guess the dingo spirit deserved some accolades too. The barking had caused me to start my ascent at the perfect time. Except for Lily and her brother, Russ insisted no other sharks lurked in the area. Better I blamed my overactive imagination on the shark anyway. I needed no reason to fear the water; I loved it too much.

Russ refused to let go of my hand while Aunt Char bandaged my arm. That she'd been waiting for me on the beach with Sandy didn't surprise me. My early morning call had scared them both. Despite having been drugged, Meryl had been awakened by the barking. She refused to say if it had been Lizzie's or the spirit's, but she'd called for help too. Even now, she stood proudly on the beach, dealing with the FBI, dressed in shorts and a misbuttoned Australian outback shirt.

The Australian Maritime Border Command picked up Lily and her brother making a run for it in *Fin's Caster* with millions of dollars in stolen diamonds. While they hadn't yet admitted to killing Lugger, Holly assured us they had prosecutable evidence. I didn't argue with her assumption that the earlier stolen diamonds were long gone.

While Holly waited, hopeful that my mother's feeling that there was more to the military angle turned up more answers, I had no doubt. Where else would I have inherited my intuition from anyway? I'd have to have a chat with Meryl eventually, but for now, Russ and I had way too much to catch up on.

That evening, Aunt Char presided over a farewell dinner at the villa that even included my mom and stepfather, who'd hitched a ride to the Cay on an FBI helicopter. They'd found the government official who'd strong-armed Holly's father into altering the military files so easily I had to wonder how the Australian Federal Police had missed it.

Although Russ and I insisted that they all stay and enjoy Canine Cay with us, everyone planned to leave in the morning. Aunt Char held up her glass. "To my darling Cat and Russ, know that no matter where your adventures take you, your back is always protected."

Not exactly what I'd expected her to say, but I toasted anyway. I got the point. Family was there for each other. No matter what.

Russ and I spent the remainder of our honeymoon on the island, exploring private beaches, diving new reefs, and enjoying each other. On our last day, I left him playing Frisbee with Lizzie and drove the EV to the Pearl Farm. It was time to discover the secret I'd been brought here to learn.

Meryl and Pearl met me in the courtyard. "Expected you sooner." I felt bad about her tentative smile. I hadn't intended to leave her hanging.

"I couldn't leave without seeing you," I said.

"I figured not." Her concern hurt. "Now that you know the Cay's secret, what will you do with it?"

"There are many secrets that are meant to be kept."

"Lugger felt the same way. Is this one of those for you?" Meryl asked.

"The Dakota Diamonds are where they belong. The giant clams protected them by turning them into even more beautiful works of art."

Meryl visibly relaxed. "The dingo spirit chose well."

"I agree. You are the true guardian, Meryl. I know this isn't the life you would've chosen, but..."

"You're wrong, Cat. This island is a part of me. It's past time for Emma and Coop to find their way, though."

The Cay without Emma and Fin? It would be tough, but Meryl was up to the challenge. "And Zed?"

"You know about that too?"

I smiled. No sense admitting to spying. "Zed couldn't have been at the A-frame on the night Lugger was murdered. The EV backing up will wake the dead. Lily knew. She'd seen Zed leave your place before dawn. It was easy for her brother to drug Lizzie and Lugger."

Meryl nodded sadly.

"It's not your fault. They've been planning this for years. Lugger didn't have a chance. None of you did," I said.

"My mind agrees, but my heart doesn't. I should've suspected," Meryl said.

"Lily was a psychopath set on revenge for what she perceived as Lugger destroying her family. No one could've known." I shuddered, remembering. I'd been there, too, only a few years ago, when I'd faced a far-too-similar situation.

"In a way, I'm surprised it took eighty years for smugglers to use oysters to hide treasure," Meryl remarked.

"How did Lily find out about the nucleation?"

Meryl shook her head. "We will likely never know for sure. I shoulda seen the signs. Lily watched Lugger like a hawk. She befriended us all in order to get closer to him."

I exhaled. There were no easy answers.

"Emma and Fin are keeping Lizzie," Meryl said.

"I thank you for that." Lizzie would always have a special place in my heart. She'd been my confidante and protector at a time when I'd been unable to help myself. Of course, she shed a whole dog a day, a big no-way for my allergy-prone husband. She also had the Energizer Bunny beat for perpetual motion. I took a long look at Pearl, Meryl's Cobberdoodle, patiently hanging on our every word. No. I had a husband to get to know first.

"What will you do with the Argyle Diamonds Lily already nucleated?" I asked.

"I can't return them without jeopardizing the safety of the Dakota Diamonds."

I knew that. "You'd better not mistakenly send them for stringing."

"Yeah. Imagine the surprise the drillers will have when they can't penetrate a pearl. I have a notion to add more museum pieces to the Cay's pearl lore."

An excellent idea. "No pressure, but I'd still love for you to consider showing the Cay Pearls in Barkview. They are a treasure that should be shared."

"I'll think 'bout it. I've something for you." Meryl handed me a small rosewood box tied with a gold ribbon. "Something to remember your adventure at Canine Cay."

"Like I'll ever forget."

"Touché."

I opened the lid. On black velvet sat the two-inch baroque clam pearl shaped like Canine Cay. My heart pounded. The piece was a jewelry lover's dream—a one-of-a-kind master-piece. "I can't accept this. It's a piece of your family's history."

"You, Cat Hawl, are family. You're the sister I choose."

Her words struck me. All the amazing women who'd touched me so profoundly came to mind. My Aunt Char, who'd nursed me both physically and mentally after that awful Pit Bull attack. Sandy, who stood by me no matter what. My mom, my half-sister, and my many Barkview buddies. This list went on.

I embraced Meryl. She was right. Blood didn't make a sister. Love did.

The End 🐾🐾🐾

I hope you enjoyed your adventure in the dog-friendliest place in America. To learn more about Barkview and Cat's next adventure, visit www.cbwilsonauthor.com.

Sign up for **The Bark View**, a monthly update on all things Barkview, including

- *Friday Funnies*: pet-related cartoons
- *WOW!* A dog did that?
- Recipes from *Bichon Bisquets Barkery's* canine kitchen
- Cool merchandise ideas from the *Bow Wow Boutique*
- Not to mention Barkview news and fun contests.

Don't miss Cat's next adventure back in Barkview when a holiday gingerbread dog house competition turns dog-eat-dog in **Dachshund to Death**.

COMING SOON:
DACHSHUND TO DEATH

A murdered pastry chef and a stolen family recipe turn Barkview's annual holiday gingerbread doghouse competition into a canine cat-astrophy.

Has this competition turned dog-eat-dog or is it something more sinister? A tent full of knife-proficient suspects complicates everything. When Sandy's sister is accused of the crime, Cat Hawl is on the scent. The deeper she digs, she realizes that the recipe itself leads to something far more valuable than the perfect holiday treat.

With the help of two devilish Dachshunds, Cat must run with the big dogs to find a 1930's treasure before the prize is eaten by time.

ACKNOWLEDGMENTS

To my writing cheerleaders Pam Wright, Dee Kaler, Becky Witters, Noel Mohberg and Brandi Wilson, who endlessly listen to my ideas, edit my spelling and grammar, help research and test recipes, thank you.

For research and police procedure assistance, thank you to Richard R. Zitzke, Chief of Police, Whitehall, Ohio, retired. I assure you any errors are entirely my fault.

Special thanks to my Aussie dialog helpers Dale Woodbridge and Anita Joy. Any errors are on me. Thank you Mary Christner and her three wonderful Aussies, JJ, Zane and Shiner. Our time together was priceless.

As always, Melissa Martin. You keep me sane.

ABOUT THE AUTHOR

The award-winning author of six Cozy Pet Mysteries and counting, C.B. Wilson's love of writing was spurred by an early childhood encounter with a Nancy Drew book where she precociously wrote what she felt was a better ending. After studying at the Gemology Institute of America, she developed a passion for researching lost, stolen and missing diamonds—the big kind. Her fascination with dogs and their passionate owners inspired Barkview, California, the dog friendliest city in America.

C.B. lives in Peoria, AZ with her husband. She is an avid pickleball player who enjoys traveling to play tournaments. She admits to chocoholic tendencies and laughing out loud at dog comics.

To connect with C.B Wilson:
www.cbwilsonauthor.com
www.facebook.com/cbwilsonauthor

AUTHOR'S NOTE

A honeymoon in Australia sounded like the perfect adventure for Cat and Russ. Canine Cay is fictional, but it was inspired by Lizard Island, located in the northern Great Barrier Reef. The missing World War II Dakota Diamonds are true. Diamonds were stolen from the Argyle mine in 2017. Their location remains unknown. Seeding oysters or giant clams with diamonds? Probably not possible.

Importing a dog, even a special show dog from the United States into Australia, is only legal after an extended quarantine. Please forgive me, but Renny couldn't be left behind.

I hope you enjoyed reading about Cat's international adventures as much as I did writing about them. After her eventful honeymoon, Cat is ready for a quiet holiday season. Unfortunately, Barkview has some secrets yet to be uncovered.

Made in the USA
Middletown, DE
27 September 2023

39301669R00109